Also by Susanna Moore

The Big Girls

THE
Big Girls

Susanna Moore

ALFRED A. KNOPF
NEW YORK 2007

To John Newman

The Big Girls

Sloatsburg Correctional Institution, a walled complex of seven large stone buildings, sits on the west bank of the Hudson River. An hour north of Manhattan by train, it was built in the late nineteenth century as a sanatorium for tuberculosis patients. Buildings A, B, and C hold five hundred prisoners of the federal government, all of them women. The remaining buildings are used for clinics, schoolrooms, the chapel, and administration as well as for the laundry, kitchens, library, and machine shop. There is a large plot of land behind Building A where the prisoners grow beans. A high brick wall with two wooden watchtowers occupied by men with rifles surrounds the prison on three sides. The river runs parallel to Building C on the east. There are no guardhouses along the river, which causes me to wonder. Do they think that black women can't swim?

My first day at Sloatsburg—six months ago this Monday— I made a cautious tour of the place, looking over my shoulder as if fearful of my own apprehension. No one seemed to notice, or to care, which I decided was a good sign. I am still making a cautious tour of the place.

I enter each weekday morning through elaborate iron gates, left from the days when Sloatsburg's population was consumptive Irish housemaids and dairy farmers, passing slowly through three security checkpoints with cameras, metal detectors, scanning machines, and electronic hand-checks to a large front hall with a white marble floor. The odor, even in the hall, is female.

My office is on the second floor of Building C. The rooms, on either side of a narrow hall, were once used by patients, but now they are occupied by the medical staff and social workers. The doors to the offices, each with a thick glass panel, are often left ajar, and it is possible to overhear the doctors and their patients. Cameras are suspended from the hall ceiling at intervals of thirty feet, although not inside the small bathroom. The bathroom is reserved for the staff. The key is one of several we are meant to keep with us at all times, along with keys to the pharmacy, clinic, file room, and chapel, which is kept locked except when it is used as a movie theater.

There are no windows in the offices. There is a wooden desk with drawers. Three metal chairs—the one with arms is for the doctor. I keep my keys in the desk, as well as a Walkman and CDs for the train ride back and forth to the city, a tape measure in a green leather case that once belonged to my mother, a penknife, tea bags, my personal drugs, an alarm clock, a photograph of my son, pens and pencils, a pencil sharpener, and some licorice. Also a flask of vodka and a map of the prison. An electric kettle, teapot, and two Japanese saké cups sit atop a file cabinet. On my desk is a cypripedium in a clay pot. Some of these things are against prison regulations. With a little reflection, I see that my small attempts to make my office more comfortable, more suitable to my tastes, are a bit spinsterish.

Each morning, after checking the pharmacy's compliance

4

sheet (expiration dates of prescriptions), I make a list of the psychiatrists' daily appointments for the officer on duty, who then arranges for the escorts to bring each patient at the appointed time. The most important events of the day are the two counts—one at ten o'clock in the morning and another at four in the afternoon. Because of the counts, there is only time to see two or three patients a day. In the past, patients were treated by a different psychiatrist every other week for a few minutes. The previous chief of staff was given large amounts of money by the government to conduct a study of the animal tranquilizer ketamine with inmates used as subjects. Ketamine induces, among other things, hallucinations, light trails, and whispering voices. I've canceled the program. If a patient is too psychotic even for us, she is taken under guard to Bellevue Hospital in Manhattan.

I am beginning to understand certain things. Appearances to the contrary, I was a nervous wreck when I arrived last fall. Louise, I would say to myself each morning, you can do this. But the truth is I didn't have a clue. It is a miracle that I've lasted this long. I still feel strained and peculiar—the foul odors, the slow black river, the bells, the yellow light, all swirling around me, make me dizzy. It is only a matter of time.

They brought me here right after my sentencing. I was pretty confused. I didn't understand I was going to be locked up for the rest of my life. I thought all along I was going to be put to death. I wanted to be put to death!

The processing took all night. I was with four other women, who I never saw again. We had to fill out a lot of forms. Then they made us take off our clothes, and they searched us like we heard they would, wearing gloves. Some of the officers wore three pairs. They kept yelling, Come on! Come on! Hurry it up, ladies, let's get this show on the road! Which made me even more nervous than I was. One of the other women was crying, and she kept saying, I am innocent, I am innocent, until a guard finally said, Oh, I guess that's why they got you all wrapped up in chains, sweetheart.

I was sweating a lot, and when I was fingerprinted, my thumb came out all blurry. When I apologized, the woman guard taking my prints said in a nice way, It's okay, hon, it's just like the first pancake. The transport officer who had drove the bus was sitting there eating Chinese food and he said, I know what you mean about that pancake. Behind him was a sign, YOU WON'T BE HOME FOR CHRISTMAS.

They asked us to wiggle our toes, pull our ears, and shake our hair, which was hard for the lady with dreads. They told us to puff out our face cheeks and our lips and to hold them that way. They sprayed us for lice and other things. Because it was so late, they decided not to give us a Pap smear and some liver tests. I kept wondering why they were going to so much trouble for people who were on their way to the electric chair, but I didn't say a word.

They put me in a big holding cell with a lot of other prisoners. It was so packed you couldn't lie down, not even on the floor. It was early in the summer, but it was already hot. There was no air-conditioning, and the hum of the generator made me feel calm, like I was inside a big machine. Some people had taken off their tops, wearing them on their head or around their waist. One lady used her bra as a headband. You were supposed to use the intercom to ask for what you needed, like a drink of water or toilet paper, but it didn't work. A lot of the women had their period and there was blood all over them. The toilet was overflowing, stuffed with all kinds of things, not just you-know-what.

They fed us at six-thirty in the morning. Lunch was at eleven, and dinner at four. After about two days—I think it was two days, I had trouble keeping track of time—I was put in my own cell. I was lucky to get moved so quick because some people are stuck there for weeks until cells are available. I found out later I wasn't even supposed to be with other women, but someone messed up. I was moved in case I was in danger. I felt bad for the ones who got left behind, but I figured they couldn't execute all of us at once. They could only do a few at a time, right? That's what I thought.

There are three psychiatrists, in addition to myself, on staff. Dr. Fischl has a full red beard and a medical degree from Grenada. Dr. Henska had her license suspended for six months in 2001 for selling human blood. Dr. de la Vega, if he is in fact a doctor, was engaged by my predecessor, who has since been promoted to Guantánamo Bay, where he advises the government on more efficient ways to increase the psychological and physical duress of prisoners. Dr. de la Vega was found through an agency called Shrinks Only. Each of the doctors has eighty patients—at least on paper. We are assisted (impeded) by three medical social workers. Ms. Morton, a case manager, was disciplined in her previous place of employment for the suicide of a twelve-year-old boy in her care. Eight locum tenentes work part-time, usually at night or on the weekend. They tend to be fourth-year psychiatric residents trying to make some money—they can earn six hundred dollars for an eight-hour shift. They have trouble staying awake.

Yesterday, I overheard Dr. Fischl and Dr. de la Vega, who wears black three-piece suits, talking about me—like my former husband, they cannot conceive why I would work in a prison. It's a good question—even I sometimes wonder why I am here. The Girl Scouts, summers with the Haida in Canada, mild lesbian attractions, and a loss of virginity at a rather late age to the regional director of Amnesty International do not in themselves account for it. Dr. Henska and Dr. de la Vega certainly wouldn't work in a prison unless compelled by reasons I hope never to know. No one wants to work as a prison doctor, except the locums. The rest of us are badly paid, although slightly better than the inmates in the psychiatric unit who earn eighteen cents an hour to keep an eye on their fellow inmates. In some institutions, they ask the more melancholy prisoners to sign a pledge that they will not kill themselves. Dr. Henska suggested in a recent staff meeting that we avail ourselves of this precaution. There is not an abundance of wit in these meetings—that would be a lot to ask—but I did think it was funny. Only when she mentioned it a second time did I realize she meant it. I looked my most puzzled, wrinkling my brow to let her know I'd changed my mind—I no longer thought it very funny. Needless to say, she dislikes me.

One hundred African American, Hispanic, and Caucasian men and women are employed by the Bureau of Prisons as corrections officers at Sloatsburg. They aren't particularly friendly to the medical staff, moving as we do between the imprisoned and their captors, and they understandably mistrust us. As do the inmates. Although both the guards and the prisoners find us a bit ridiculous, there is a collective understanding that it does no harm to indulge us. You never know when a doctor might come in handy. The wilier of both groups manipulate us at their pleasure. It is every man for himself. Not the prisoners, but the medical staff.

Once I was put in my own cell, they took away the orange jumpsuit I wore in court and gave me two pairs of used jeans, four used black T-shirts in different sizes, black sneakers with elastic sides that fit perfect, three pairs of white tube socks, three pairs of white cotton underpants, two bras, a new blue sweatshirt, and a used black sweater. That's when it began to dawn on me maybe I wasn't going to die. And that's when I REALLY got crazy.

My patient Helen appears to be better. Of course, almost anything is an improvement over last month when she was found naked at the door of her cell, shouting Swim away, Ariel! Swim away! Three officers wrapped her in a suicide blanket as heavy as lead and carried her to the psychiatric unit, where she was kept for three weeks. I've had to change her prescription—fifteen milligrams of Haldol with four hundred fifty milligrams of Effexor, three hundred milligrams of Wellbutrin for depression, and a little Cogentin for the side effects of the Haldol. She is back in her own cell in Building C now.

There was some concern when she arrived last summer that her life was in danger, and she was kept in special housing for her own safety. (Last year, an inmate who had watched her husband beat her seven-year-old daughter to death after forcing the child to eat cat food and defecate in kitty litter was found drowned in her toilet bowl.) It eventually became apparent that no one intended to harm Helen, primarily because she was under the protection of an inmate named Wanda, and she was allowed to enter the general population. Her friendship with Wanda makes everything easier for her. I find Wanda a little frightening. I hope that she's not manipulating Helen to use her for illegal commissions. Some of the more aggressive inmates employ the mentally ill and other particularly powerless inmates for criminal purposes, as they aren't unduly punished if caught.

Helen asked me during our session today if I could bring her a subscription form to a handicraft magazine, as she wishes to start thinking about her Christmas gifts. I was sorry to have to refuse, but it is against the rules. She asks for so little, unlike the other women.

They make it hard for us prisoners. Not that I have any complaints. It's just not that easy to hide your meds in your mouth when the aide sticks her rubber fingers down your throat three times a day. I broke my glasses last month, but all that got me was three days in ad seg. Now they're held together with Snoopy Band-Aids. I still can't have pens, pencils, or a mirror. No hair dryer, wand for heating water, or curling iron for me. Anything with a cord, basically. I can't even have a plastic rosary—I doubt I could hang myself with a rosary.

I can't say I blame them. I almost killed myself when I was fifteen, which means I almost succeeded, not that I thought about it and decided not to. I took three bottles of Coricidin, but I threw up in the back of my mom's car. There was red all over the place, and she figured out what it was, even though I always got carsick. It's not fun, I can tell you, to have your stomach pumped. They make it hurt as much as they can so you won't do it again. They're busy with real problems and it's a lot of trouble for them. It's not like you were in a motorcycle accident or you really have something wrong with you. I was in the state hospital for a month after that. I refused to see my mother and Uncle Dad until I figured out it was working against me. I wanted to get out so I could do it again. I would have done it again, too, but I met Jimmy and everything changed for a while.

The new doctor sometimes comes by in the morning to see how I'm doing. Her name is Dr. Forrest. She smiled at me today. It's because of how my glasses look, I think. I came right out and asked her why she was smiling, and she said, You look charming.

No one ever told me I looked charming before. It confused me. Then she said my new medicine would make me feel different. It is a time-release so my moods will not be all over the place. I told her I already feel different, and she asked could I describe it. It's not depression, I said, if that's what you're thinking. It's DOUBT. That's the only thing I can call it. She said the better the medicine works, the sadder I'll feel. Which I'd of said was not a possibility. I'm not on suicide watch anymore so I guess I'm not better. If I was better, I'd have to kill myself. She said if things go okay, which they seem to be doing, I'll get my measuring book and ruler and pens back.

Helen is a twenty-eight-year-old woman of Scotch-Irish and Polish descent. She grew up in a working-class family on Long Island, New York. She has one sibling, a younger brother named Kelly, who serves in the United States Army. Previous to her recent incarceration, she had no criminal record, although she has a substantial psychiatric history. She has succeeded in cutting herself twice since her arrival at the prison last June, using the lenses of her glasses and the crucifix of a rosary. Her thin forearms are ringed with old and new scars.

As she expected, even wished, to be put to death for her crime, she believes that her sentence is not sufficiently severe. She has subsequently devised her own means of punishment, which is to eat as little as possible, at the same time satisfying a craving for sugar. She lives on Sno-Caps candy, eating three to four boxes a day. (She told me that if she could have one wish in the world it would be to eat pizza with her son Shane.) She will not touch the packages of food that her mother occasionally sends, but gives them to other inmates. I've discussed her diet with a prison doctor, Dr. Subramaniya, but short of feeding her by force, there is nothing that can be done. I've requested that she be given an eye exam. She is very attached to her glasses, which are broken, cleaning them frequently with that solemn concern demonstrated by people who have worn glasses since childhood.

There was something in my face, perhaps, or in my voice when she spoke of her children today that caused her to ask if I, too, had children. Of course, I couldn't answer her. She rarely speaks of her husband, who is a Pentecostal Christian, except to say that he must hate her. I would hate myself if I knew me, she said.

L ast night, a girl named Frankie was dragged past my cell on her way to solitary. They say she was running a gambling casino. She was screaming the whole way, Tell that motherfucking cunt-sucking whore Charlene I am going to fuck her ass up BAD when I come back! and someone yelled, You ain't never coming back, baby. There were screams of laughter up and down the tier. I admit I smiled.

I see Helen once a week in private session. She has been my patient for five months now. I find her a little repellent. I'm ashamed of that. She was in the habit of urinating and defecating on the floor of her cell, and the smell used to make me gag, but she is using the toilet now. (Freud believed that women were first designated guardians of the hearth because they could not urinate on fire to put it out, a compulsion, it appears, that no man can resist.) I cannot tell if my repugnance is due to her crime or her character—perhaps it is the same thing. At the very least she has led me back to Bettelheim—Djuna Barnes writes that children really like to see the wolf and Red Riding Hood in bed together.

The Big Girls, as Captain Bradshaw calls us, can be very original with their outfits, but I wear the same thing every day. The jeans and the T-shirt and the sneakers, with the added touch of the sweater when needed—it's so cold, I've been wearing the sweater every day. I've lost weight, and my jeans are a little loose without a belt. My friend Wanda refuses to wear a bra, which wouldn't bother most people, especially men, but it bothers me, mainly cause I don't know where to look. Another person, who will be nameless, wears her sweatshirt like a pair of shorts with her legs stuffed into the arms. Wanda pulls her socks way up which is a sign of you-know-what. There was a time not so long ago when I wasn't changing my clothes, or using the toilet, and I guess it got pretty bad. It was the new doctor that helped me out of that one.

As chief of psychiatry at Sloatsburg, I receive many promotional brochures from prisons around the country: "Niantic, Connecticut, is home to the only women's prison in the state. The Farm, as it was once called, was a state work farm and prison for prostitutes, unwed mothers, and other women of immoral character. If convicted today of an offense the state deems worthy of confinement, be it minor violation or mass murder, the prisoner will find herself in an unbelievable environment with impressive security features few male prisons can boast."

An elderly clerk in the records office told me that the immoral women at Niantic used to fish from a bridge on the property and fry up their catch at night, but no longer. A mother was allowed to keep a child born in prison for a year after its birth, but that practice has also been stopped. Women were imprisoned at Niantic for the crime of lascivious carriage until the late sixties, when it was at last ruled unconstitutional.

Last night a voice in my cell kept shouting, Peace perfect peace in this dark world of sin, the blood of Jesus whispers, Peace within. It was so loud I sat up and put my hands over my ears. If you asked me, Who is the voice, I would say it varies. It's not like hearing the Little Mermaid tell me to Swim swim away, and then she herself swims away! Sometimes the voice is my friend Ellie, and sometimes it is my Messengers. The Horsemen.

Ellie has been giving me advice since I was in the fourth grade. That was when I first had thoughts about suicide, and Ellie talked me out of it. She is two years older than me, and we became friends because of our love for elephants. I trust Ellie. I never really needed anyone else once I found her. Whenever I had to do something really bad, something I just couldn't do myself, Ellie would do it for me. She never let me down. She always understood what I had to do, and she never made me feel sad. It's funny but she didn't believe me about the Messengers at first, maybe because she couldn't see them. She couldn't SMELL them, either. They have a terrible smell of burning teeth. They came the first time right after we moved in with Uncle Dad. I was sick with the measles, and I thought I was dreaming. The Messengers wouldn't come if Uncle Dad was in the room.

My patient Helen is courteous, ordinary, shy. Although without education, she is not ignorant. She knows that she is worthy of interest. She understands what she has done—she is incapable of evasion—and it causes her anguish. She rarely smiles, but when she does, she holds her mouth tightly shut to hide the gap of a missing bottom tooth knocked out by her brother Kelly in a childhood accident. She often closes her eyes when she speaks, as if to hide from sight all that she has done, and yet she hasn't the slightest interest in defending or even explaining herself. When she speaks of her crime, she becomes disoriented, stopping in the middle of a sentence, short of breath. (I wonder if my inability to take notes fast enough is because of the erratic nature of her thoughts, or because I myself am mesmerized. I mentioned this to my analyst, who, good boy that he is, said nothing. I have learned to discern certain of his thoughts by the subtlest changes in his breathing, but, in this instance, he gave away nothing.) Sometimes she will stop speaking abruptly, her head cocked as if listening to a voice that cautions her to silence. An altogether closed person. Just my type.

As she grows more lucid, she becomes more despondent. The suggestion that the voices she hears may have been imagined leaves her frightened and confused. Her hallucinations, those terrifying substitutes for other desires long lost to consciousness, have not occurred in seven weeks. Or so she says. I doubt that they have stopped altogether. As Professor Cluff used to say, over and over again, as if I could ever forget: The unconscious never sleeps.

I guess you could say Dr. Forrest is a mystery to me. The other day she mentioned very relaxed that someone named Saint Teresa heard voices, and I knew she meant was I hearing voices again. I wanted to say, I know what you're thinking, Dr. Forrest, but I didn't because then she would know I could READ HER MIND. Not that I have special powers or anything. I just knew that's what she meant, but she didn't want to come right out and say it because she is a very considerate person. For some people, there is a separation between their inside and outside self, but in a good way. I imagine she is like that. I am the opposite, at least for now. It's nice for me. It shouldn't be nice but it is, because there is NO SEPARATION between my inner and outer part. There is no difference at all.

. . .

17

I saw my former husband, Rafael Rivera, for the first time late one night in the CPEP at Bellevue Hospital. I was one of the doctors on call. He was holding in his arms a skinny teenager whose head had just exploded from a surfeit of methamphetamine. She had vomited on his brown-and-white shoes, and I asked the psych tech to bring him a towel to clean them. I learned later that the tech, a good-looking Dominican boy, followed Rafael outside to give him his phone number. Rafael's unexpected blend of reserve and tenderness was very appealing to me. Appealing to all of us, it seems, but I was dying of loneliness, which I wouldn't have suspected of the Dominican. I told Rafael that I needed his number in case the girl did not survive. He was so gentle with her, so attentive and assured, that I thought they were lovers, but they had only met that afternoon. The girl didn't die, but I waited two days before I called him.

I was on my way to the Met to see a show of Rubens drawings, and I asked him if he'd like to meet me there. If he was surprised by my invitation, he gave no sign of it. We met in the galleries. He took his time before each drawing. I'd been a student of the eccentric Professor Wollheim at Berkeley, notorious for spending hours in front of a painting—it was not uncommon for someone to report him to a museum guard as the gentleman paralyzed before the Poussin—so I was not deterred by Rafael's pace. I wondered, with a pleasant shock, watching his narrow shoulders in his green jacket, if he was trying to impress me. When I found myself staring at the back of his neck, his dark hair as oily and tight as Persian lamb, I blushed. I found out later he wasn't trying to impress me—it was just something he did. He hadn't been to college, and he was educating himself.

We finally left the museum, and he walked me home through the park. He didn't say much, and I didn't, either.

I was surprised three days later when he called to ask if we could have a drink. Before sleeping with me, he went through my closet and threw out all of my awful catalog clothes—a garbage bag stuffed with brown corduroy shifts and hemp drawstring trousers. A week later, he arranged for a friend of his, a costume designer, to take me shopping at Barneys. Tight skirts and a pair of black patent-leather high heels. Apparently he had a fantasy about the high heels and a white lab coat, but the docs in the psych ward don't wear white coats. Too dangerous.

I can tell Dr. Forrest doesn't have the same background as me, even though we sort of look the same. We're both on the skinny side. We both have straight brown hair to our shoulders. Our eyes are brown. She doesn't pluck her eyebrows, and I don't, either. Sometimes I put my hair in a braid like hers, now that they gave back my rubber bands. She speaks very soft, which is the real giveaway. No one in my house ever spoke that way. You yelled all the time if you wanted anyone to hear you. I can tell Dr. Forrest never had to yell. Sometimes it gets on my nerves, like she thinks she is better than me, even if I know she doesn't really think that. Everything is a little slowed down when Dr. Forrest is around—May I? Will you? Would you please? I'm not used to that. I could get used to it, though.

. . .

In our staff meeting this morning, Dr. Fischl, scratching his beard noisily, complained that the restrictions for women prisoners are more petty than they would be for men, which he finds unjust, as women do not usually consider a shank whittled from a comb to make a suitable birthday present. Dr. Fischl was for five years a psychiatrist at Attica Correctional Facility. It was at Attica that forty-three men were killed in a riot in 1971. I find him quite strange. Of course, there are all kinds of strangeness.

Male prisoners, according to Dr. Fischl, are instructed not to speak outside the group about their therapy sessions because too much communal discussion of their crimes is thought to evoke a masturbatory excitement that would compel them, were they not constrained by imprisonment, to rush out to sodomize and strangle a child, preferably at the same time. Women would appear not to experience such excitement, which is fortunate, as it is common knowledge that they cannot be compelled to silence, unlike men.

Dr. Fischl claims that since September 11, tapes of Yoko Ono, played over and over again, are used by military intelligence to reduce intransigent terrorists to obedience, and he wonders if the tapes might be of use here. When I asked if he found torture to be particularly effective in the treatment of the incarcerated, he wiggled his beard at me—it has always been difficult for me to know when I am being teased.

It is melancholy today. The fog laps the banks of the river and there is a brackish smell at low tide. Water seeps through the walls. Everything is damp. The heaters I requested for my office have not arrived, and I keep blankets in the file cabinet for the women to wrap around themselves.

. . .

My cell is tiny, but that's because it's for one person only. It has hooks on the wall for my wardrobe and a built-in table with a stool screwed to the floor. The hooks are always falling off, but that's so you can't use them to hang yourself. There's a metal plank attached to the wall for a bed, and a mattress and a pillow. There's a metal sink and toilet in the corner, and a locker—half a locker, really—to keep your personal belongings in. Anything that can't fit inside the locker is confiscated. There are three nice shelves above the bed. A fluorescent light is cemented to the wall.

My first night, I heard the person in the cell next to me, which turns out was Sessilee, say, These cells get smaller every year. I wouldn't know about that. I wasn't thinking about anything except my kids. I really missed them. I had a pain in my chest where my heart would be, and it still hasn't gone away. I hope it doesn't ever go away. That's how I know I'm not dead.

When I am feeling overwhelmed, I take a deep breath (and a Klonopin) and obediently return to the Signs and Symptoms. I remind myself that I am a physician. I am the mother of an eight-year-old boy. I am not an inmate. I have not embezzled the Ladies' Garment Workers' pension fund or killed my common-law husband with a George Foreman grill. I take comfort in the fact that few of my patients are psychotic. You have to be really out of your mind for a prison psychiatrist to render a diagnosis of schizophrenia, perhaps because an insane person is not supposed to be executed—I am in the curious position of attempting to restore a poor soul to her right mind so that the state can kill her with a clear conscience. Apparently, it's not great for dentists, either. Dr. Fischl told me that a murderer executed last month in Texas had a root canal the morning of his execution. I'm not sure that I believe him. I'm not sure that I'm meant to believe him. Despite his oddness, there is something comforting about Dr. Fischl.

There was snow this afternoon. It was LOVELY, or so Dr. Forrest would say in her funny way. I wouldn't really know. She is trying to get me interested in things, like the weather, which is a weird idea in this place. Spring is definitely NOT in the air, she says. She is like a bird in spring herself, her brown eyes sparkling, so I guess she would know if it's in the air or not.

I would know if I looked out the window, but I don't have one, and she doesn't, either. I haven't been out of bed except to measure the legs of the chair a few times. I feel much better now that I have my measurement book and my ruler and pens, though they didn't return my tape, which means I can't measure anything that is round. I've tried doing it with a ruler and it just doesn't work. I wonder if it was Dr. Forrest who got my supplies returned. I asked her and she denied it, but I think it was. The officer who took my book told me she thought it was just scribbling, and she almost threw it out!

Dr. Forrest was staring at my arms again today. She said the pain of cutting is a relief when you've lost all other feeling—people cut theirselves so they know they are ALIVE. That's not why I cut myself. I have other ways I know I'm alive, but I didn't tell her that. She tries to be cool about it. She doesn't say, How do you cut yourself, Helen? She says, How's your skin doing? Believe me, I told her, it is NOT easy to cut yourself in prison, which made her smile. I like it when I can make her smile, but I wasn't kidding. It's not easy when you aren't allowed a sharp instrument. Once I bent that little catch on a Hello Kitty barrette, but I can't say it got the job done.

My arms are really ugly from all the cuts. Jo, who is Wanda's wife, gives me some of the peanut oil she uses for cooking to rub on them. One reason they look so bad is each time they put the stitches in, I pull them out. I left the last ones in, but only because I'm scared of the night nurse. If you saw her, you'd be scared, too. I know one of the reasons Dr. Forrest is having confidence in me is I didn't take out the last stitches, but I didn't tell her it was because of the nurse. If Dr. Forrest thinks I'm getting better, I don't want to talk her out of it. I told her I was glad to be off suicide watch, and she said she was glad, too.

The first thing I do when I come home from the prison is take a bath, convinced that its very atmosphere suffuses my hair and my skin. I asked my son Ransom tonight if I smelled bad, and he said that I did not, but, to my surprise, he asked if he could sit with me while I bathed. As he rinsed my back, he told me for the twentieth time that his father has a pool in California and a blue parrot.

Now I can hear him in his room, playing with the plastic action figures (Richard Coeur de Lion, Saladin, and various foot soldiers from different centuries) that Rafael sends him, which explains the cries of warfare coming down the hall. Unlike his mother, he tends to identify with the winner. Last year for Ransom's birthday, Rafael, who was in New York for a music video, had a miniature plywood fort complete with drawbridge made for him, small enough to fit inside Ransom's bedroom and sturdy enough to hold a young boy. Ransom is very happy in his fort. It makes him feel small and powerful. I assume that it makes his father feel powerful, too.

I like my little household. Mother Bear. Baby Bear. And Evelyn. Evelyn is from Haiti. She is the sister of one of the psychiatric nurses who looked after me when I was locked up in Payne Whitney. She has been with us since Ransom was a baby. She has two children of her own and I encourage her to bring them to play with Ransom. He doesn't like them. The truth is he doesn't really like anyone but me. Once Evelyn discovered that Ransom was learning French at the Lycée—something I'd tried to keep from her—she insisted on speaking to him in patois, as I knew she would. Unfortunately, she is incomprehensible. He is grateful to see me each evening in part because I am a diversion from the strain of her attention. I don't know what we'd do without Evelyn.

D r. Forrest got me a eye exam from the outside eye doctor and I already have brand-new glasses! No more Snoopy Band-Aids! Keesha says she waited six months for her bifocals to come. My eyes are a little sensitive, maybe cause there's no sunlight here. They are really nice for prison glasses. Everyone gets the same pair—thin, not too big, and clear. Dr. Forrest complimented me on them. They're a little like her glasses, now that I think of it. Like a lot of plain people, I have nice eyes.

. . .

I see twenty-five of the women each week in private session, among them Darla, Keesha, Jolene, Shaynna, Aida, Tiffany, Wanda, Shirley, and LizAnn. As most of the medical files have been misplaced or lost—many never existed in the first place—it is difficult to instigate a treatment consistent with a patient's history. Some of the women have not been treated for psychiatric or physical ailments in more than two years. We are always starting from scratch.

Medicine was previously distributed in a haphazard if not dangerous way, and I've introduced a seemingly novel system, at least when it comes to narcotics, of locks and ledgers. I've requested that a dentist be hired, but so far without success. Many of the women suffer from terrible tooth pain. More than half of all deliberately inflicted trauma is to the head and neck, and many of the inmates have crushed teeth and jaws from years of domestic beatings.

One of my patients, Keesha, is here for robbing a man and stealing his SUV after they had sexual intercourse in the front seat of his car. She likes to talk about it. She cleaned herself with some dirty paper napkins from Burger King that she found in the glove compartment. She thought at first that there was blood on the napkins, which excited her, but then she realized that it was ketchup. Which is when she used the gun she also found in the glove compartment. She didn't have much to say today because of the pain of a burn; Sessilee is spending four days in administrative segregation for scalding her in a jealous rage. Dr. Subramaniya doesn't believe that Keesha will need a skin graft, which is fortunate, as she is an unusually ugly woman. Keesha said the burn turned out to be a good thing because of all the

Vicodin she's been prescribed. She needs the extra money she makes from selling the pills to other inmates.

I've noticed that many of my patients refer to their victims by their first names, as if they were members of their family or even lovers. The more extreme the offense, the more intimate the relationship. A young girl named Dawn, here for two hundred months for shooting a bystander in a robbery, refers to the victim, an elderly woman, as my darling granny. Darla is convinced that her boyfriend's murdered wife, whom she did not know, was her sister.

The prisoners are very secretive. The occasional scapegoat from outside (the minister, the social worker, the new prisoner) only enhances their instinctive resistance. Their acute awareness of their separateness encourages a sense of superiority and makes it difficult, in most instances, to leave prison for the greater, if less encompassing, world that awaits them. Of course, their troubles are not over when they leave and often ensure their return. I will never penetrate this spellbound place.

I get pretty jumpy when I run out of things to measure. There isn't much in my cell to begin with, and I've measured everything four or five times. I even measured the ruler. What I'm doing now is I'm measuring everything all over again, only in meters.

My cell is in the middle of the row, and I can see a little on each side through the glass in the door. I watch the guards as close as they watch me. Closer. It's like standing on the corner watching the world go by. Sometimes they are taking someone to the clinic, or to court, or to a meeting with their lawyer. People have their very own sounds—footsteps, coughs, rude remarks—and there are strange smells, too, not just Pine-Sol or cooking smells, but the smell of something rotten. Dead animals, maybe.

One of the guards, Officer M. Rossi, wears real strong amounts of perfume. Liz Claiborne, Shaynna says. Shaynna can smell her coming. She says Officer Rossi wears it on purpose to drive her wild. I wouldn't know about that. Shaynna says the smell of cigarettes on officers just starting their shifts makes her so crazy she could eat a newspaper. Shaynna is in a cell on my left side with Sessilee, and Keesha is on the other side with Aida, Kai, Maribel, and Jazmeen in what they call a cell dorm. They have little desks and little chairs and beds, just like Snow White and the Seven Dwarfs, only there are five of them.

Feeling better can make you WANT something to happen and that can lead you to MAKE it happen. Sometimes I catch Dr. Forrest looking at me funny over the top of her glasses. I feel bad about the things I keep from her, but it's really for her own good. I think for her sake it's better to go slow. I don't have to tell her EVERYTHING. It wouldn't be good for her.

Sometimes I think about the other women she sees and try to guess who she likes best. She has a lot to choose from. It seems like the women who have gone as far as they can are the nicest. The ones strung out on drugs with their big personalities scare you to death. The ones who cut their grandfathers to pieces seem like pussycats compared to them.

Dr. Forrest talks about my integration, which makes me

sound black. She said today they might move me cause they need the smaller cells for difficult prisoners. I guess that means I'm not difficult anymore. I don't want to get my hopes up.

I look at my e-mail every morning when I arrive at the prison. Today Rafael forwarded me an article from a Web site about Susan Smith: "A man behind the wheel of his pickup was not intoxicated late last Sunday when his truck rolled into the lake where Susan Smith drowned her sons. Marshal Doug Tucker said no drugs were found in the body of twenty-six-year-old Scoop Alberson, and there was no evidence of a heart condition in the tragedy that took the lives of Mr. Alberson and the four children in his vehicle on their visit to the popular lakeside shrine. Michael and Alex Smith were drowned there by their mother Susan Smith in 1994. Two oversized teddy bears were found in the cab of the truck and investigators believe they were presents for the deceased Smith children. Mr. Alberson's wife and another woman also drowned in the incident. Marshal Tucker was hoping to interview the mechanic who recently did work on the truck."

That Rafael has the time to send me hundreds of clippings and e-mails would suggest that he has accommodated the many demands of his own busy career in Los Angeles. It would also suggest that he misses me, a possibility that only occasionally gives me pleasure. He still cannot understand why I passed up the chance of a good Park Avenue practice in order to treat incarcerated junkies, whores, and murderers on behalf of the federal government. There is no profit in it, he says, and, worse, no style, a dismissal which illustrates his belief that one's work should be a source of beauty as well as profit. I admire his standards, but my interests lie elsewhere. (When I told Professor Cluff that I was going to work in a prison, he laughed out loud. Aren't we taking our conscience a bit seriously? he asked.)

I finally wrote the letter! She was on the *Today* show last week to talk about her movie, and there was a article in *People* about her, too. She's doing a pilot for HBO—that girl will not have a minute to read a letter, let alone write one. It will be a miracle if I hear from her. The article says her nickname is the Most Wavishing Wactwess in Howwywood—she has a little speech problem, which she says she's working on. She's petite with long blonde hair and blue eyes. In other words, gorgeous. All natural. She was born in April, that lovely month of diamonds and daisies. 1984. I was four years old. That is the year I learned to ride a bike.

In my letter, I said I didn't want one single thing from her except a friend in need. She'll find that hard to believe, I know, but only time will show I mean what I say. Even if she wanted to do something for me, I would not take a thing. I explained that all I want is a little note saying she got my letter and that she knows. That would be enough for me. I tucked a photo of Kaley and Shane in the letter.

My mom's only request is to leave her out of it completely. Which is not easy, considering. But I promised and I will keep my promise. A promise is a promise, not that my mom keeps them. You'd think, things being the way they are, my mom would want to be included in this. It sounds mean to say, but you'd think she'd want something out of it, like a house. She says she doesn't, and I tend to believe her, cause why didn't she write all these years. She said, That girl doesn't want to hear from the likes of you, even if you are famous. She'll be ashamed to have anything to do with you. Besides, she says it's all in my imagination. Like always.

I can only pray she is wrong.

I had LizAnn, Shaynna, Keesha, Darla, Kai, Mary, and Aida in group session this afternoon. We used to meet in the dayroom at five o'clock after the work details were finished, but the outrage of the women watching television was understandably so great that I convinced the warden that he should let us meet in an empty storeroom. The room was once used to bottle maple syrup, and the faint aroma of the syrup is very soothing. We regress immediately to an imaginary but fragrant morning in childhood.

Darla informed us today that as soon as the humans have their life essences extracted by the owl queen who lives on Venus, her conviction will be reversed. Should she be wrong about this, Darla will be spending the next forty-three years with us for her enthusiastic part in the dismemberment of her boyfriend's wife. Convicted of murder in the first degree, kidnapping, tampering with evidence, and perjury, she has a disconcerting habit of preening before a small plastic mirror that she keeps in her pocket. She has a lovely face, with long black hair that she wears loose. I certainly cannot fault her for admiring herself.

Darla finds the truth somewhat arbitrary, having the ease of brutality that comes with an absence of guilt. She is one of the few patients I have who is clinically remorseless. She does not deny her crime, and she feels no sorrow or regret. She would do it again tomorrow if she had the chance. She claims in her logical way that there was no premeditation in her act—more than that, there was no malice. Afore or after. The machete that cut her boyfriend's wife to pieces belonged to the owl queen. Darla could not possibly take credit for something so divinely effective. There was a dead woman, yes, but no way was she murdered.

Aida, a plump, untidy Guatemalan with a mustache, caught my eye with a conspiratorial smile while Darla was describing the owl queen (hair extensions, tattoos, Chanel platform shoes). I recognize my culpability in meeting Aida's glance, and I must be more circumspect. For someone who suffers from hypervigilance, I have been uncustomarily lax these last few months. When Aida said to me, Yo soy muy avergonzada de esta mujer, I should not have nodded. Aida is adept at forming alliances, I can see, and I am growing susceptible to joining them. I am growing susceptible to a lot of things.

Aida escaped eleven years ago from a work furlough while confined to a juvenile detention center. She had stabbed a girl, her cousin, at school. After her escape, she was on the street for four years before she was arrested for shoplifting, when it was discovered that she was a juvenile escapee, although no longer a minor. She says that she misses using crack because it makes her life simple—with crack she is either stoned or in jail. Being a junkie saved her life by giving her a reason to live. She has a terrible temper. She wears the Serenity Prayer on a string around her neck. After her hour with me, she goes to a meeting organized by a local Twelve-Step group. She also belongs to a charismatic Christian sect from El Salvador that impatiently awaits the Imminence of the Rapture. Because of this, she claims not to believe in the collection of any waste, and she receives endless infraction slips for the condition of her bunk. I was bewildered at first by her refusal to clean, until Dr. de la Vega pointed out that a messier planet is that much closer to the end.

I had a coffee with him today in the canteen. He made me smile when he said, Schizophrenia is my soft spot. I wonder if he exaggerates the potential for danger just to scare me. He has been here for two years, however, and I have been here only seven months. Some of the inmates are members of the Aryan Sisterhood, transferred from a penitentiary in northern California when they attacked three women in a laundry room with hot irons, burning one of them fatally. Captain Bradshaw, the officer in charge of Building C, is said to call them the Ku Klux Klitties.

My friend Wanda mailed the letter to Hollywood on her way to services. They say she goes to church to sell drugs, but I wouldn't know about that. My observation period won't be officially terminated till next Friday, so I had to get a stamp from her, too.

Wanda says she'll write back because I'm famous, and famous people like other famous people. The trouble is Wanda thinks I WANT SOMETHING, which I don't. It's hard for people to think you could do something for nothing. It doesn't make sense to them. Like one little stamp for ten Kotex. I'd have given Wanda two hundred Kotex and she knew it. I asked her not to tell anybody about the letter.

If she mailed it like she said, then it will get there by next Monday, I am guessing, which is five days, counting half a day Saturday, and Sunday when the post office is closed. It should take another week to get from California back to New York, which means I might, underline might, hear from her in twenty-two days, counting a few days for her to get over the shock, which would make it February 2.

Yesterday afternoon on my way to see a patient, an Officer Cready stopped me to ask if I'd like to join him for a couple of Zins after work. I thought at first that he was referring to a new medication—for an instant an image of us in the parking lot throwing back little paper cups of antipsychotics flashed before me. Cready, a fat man in his fifties, wears an inky black hairpiece, which gives him a sly, dishonest look. As he walks on tiptoe, it makes for a somewhat theatrical effect, particularly when he flashes his teeth.

He wanted to know if I'd like to stop by the Annex, a bar not far from the prison. I was so disconcerted that I said no. I could have kicked myself. It wouldn't hurt to be friends with these men. I might even learn something. I spent quite a bit of time with corrections officers when I was a graduate student at Stanford, administering questionnaires in Folsom Prison (Do you believe that a murderer has lost the right to live? Yes or no), so I have some experience with this kind of person.

When I declined his invitation, he said, Well, that's a shame—I just happen to have the Tip of the Month for you.

I suggested that he give it to me anyway.

After a moment's hesitation, he said, You can never go wrong locking a door. And don't slam it when you do.

I thanked him, and asked him to keep me in mind for February.

Wanda dropped off some new magazines for me on her recreation break. If you don't hide your magazines here, they get stolen pretty fast. I lost some just the other day. Dr. Forrest was the only other person around, but it couldn't of been her.

Now that I'm off observation, I'll get back my pj's with the elastic waist, instead of having to wear a paper jumpsuit. They won't let you wear nightgowns here cause when you sleep they ride up and your body is exposed for all to see. Sessilee, my next-door neighbor, sleeps on top of her covers summer and winter so she never has to make her bed. You would definitely not want to see Sessilee exposed. I already got my orange plastic shoes back, and they are hanging in a net bag from my door, the only spot of color, which they say is a good decorating trick.

. . .

An inmate named Dakota was dragged hysterical to my office this morning after a recently hired corrections officer discovered her feeding a live mouse to her pet iguana, Betsy K., a popular resident of the prison for the last seven years. Dakota was put into handcuffs, and Betsy K. and the mouse were finally flushed down the toilet after numerous tries, when Dakota collapsed onto the floor of her cell with a seizure. I gave Dakota eight hundred milligrams of Tegretol and sent her back to her cell. Building C, where Dakota lives, has been renamed Jurassic Park.

My new medicine makes me a little zonked out. It's hard to remember all the things I am trying to know now. Things I am trying to know for Dr. Forrest. It's like I want to give my feelings to her as a present.

I told her about Ellie. It was a big decision for me. It fills me with sadness just to say Ellie's name. Dr. Forrest said when a child is hurt like I was, the pain gets all confused with excitement, especially if the child thinks that special someone loves her. Or needs her. It hurts at first, and then she likes it. It begins to feel good. The body really can't help itself, Dr. Forrest said. I understood what she was saying, and later it made me cry.

I'm tired now, but I can't sleep. Dr. Forrest wears me out. I wish Ellie was here to put me to sleep. They still haven't given me back my bottles, but there is a plastic tube with some shampoo in it. I will shove it up till it hurts.

. . .

When administering the standardized 730 exam to determine if a defendant is too insane to be tried, I am required to ask: What is the purpose of a judge? What is the purpose of a jury? What will be the consequences if you are found guilty? What will be the consequences if you are found not guilty?

I was so ignorant when I began working here that I took my patient Keesha's boast that she had brothers, a grandmother, aunts, and a grandfather in detention as literal truth, appalled by yet another example of the breakdown of the family—I had yet to discover the intricate kinship of the prison family. I've made a little progress since then—that would be unavoidable—but I remain so ignorant that it embarrasses me. When I heard Helen screaming at the door of her cell for Ariel, I thought that she was referring to the spirit in *The Tempest*. I only discovered recently that Helen's Ariel is the mermaid in Disney's *The Little Mermaid*.

She told me today about Ellie. It is Ellie who has always done the things she literally could not bear to do. It was Ellie who would go in her place to her stepfather. She told me that when she was ten years old, she and Ellie ran away. Her stepfather chased after them. When they climbed a tree to get away from him, he grabbed a buzz saw and cut down the tree.

What happened then? I asked. I don't remember, she said, her eyes shut tight.

The Messengers first arrived when she was six years old, soon after her mother married Mr. Scanlon. It was Ellie who gave her the strength to live until her children were born.

·   ·   ·

I'm kind of fascinated by this lady in New York who sent me the letter from prison, even if she's out of her fucking mind! I can't believe it made it all the way to L.A. She knows everything about me! I was on the *Today* show right before Christmas to do publicity for my film, and she saw me on it. Mr. Gerald Sharp, my legal representative, wants to send her a letter. He says it's his responsibility as my attorney, plus he wants it on record. Her letter didn't seem that bad to me, certainly not life defying, but he doesn't want me to have anything to do with her, in public or private. I wish I'd talked to her before I did that TV remake of *The Snake Pit*, but c'est la vie. It says in the magazines the medicine she takes for her hallucinations makes her pretty sane now. She did the horrible thing she did because voices told her to.

She claims we are united in sisterhood, which is pretty scary when you think about it. She included a picture of her two sad-looking kids, which gave me the creeps. She's such a fan I'd send her some of my films even if Gerry would flip out, but I wonder, Do they have DVDs in prisons yet? Anyway she says she doesn't want anything from me, we are all the same under the sun, some of us lost but now we are found, blah, blah, blah. Well, speak for yourself, I wanted to say.

The last time I was in New York City was after September 11 when Deidra did a benefit and I went with her, which is how I ended up with Eddie Joyce and his girlfriend Mandy in my guest bedroom for five months. When Deidra met Eddie, she said, Oh my God, he's so Nassau County, which turns out was a compliment. He needed to get out of New York after everything that happened, so he and Mandy came back with us on Deidra's plane to L.A. and they stayed until Rafael moved in. I never told

Rafael what was going on, just that Eddie was this fireman from New York who was freaked out by all his friends dying in the Twin Towers.

We had a good time while it lasted. I introduced him and Mandy to Tussionex, which I get by the carton from Dr. Kupper—anything I really like is a triplicate. I only take drugs to change my reality. The coke takes me up, and the vodka takes me over—abracadabra, there's my new reality. The bad part is it only lasts a few hours, which is where the Tussionex comes in. I taught Mandy how to do cough syrup and she taught me how to cook a ham with coke, as in Coca-Cola. She's from Florida. Forget the pineapple and brown sugar, that girl knew how to bake a ham. Eddie'd never done cough syrup before, although he'd done everything else. Firemen will try just about anything it turns out, not only drugs. In the end, all anyone wants, not just firemen, is two things—get rid of the anxiety and get euphoric, which you might think is the same, but it's not. When you do anything new, there's euphoric, at least in the beginning, and that's what I was able to give Eddie Joyce. I have a whole chemical routine worked out which I developed over the years: three and a half Vicodins spaced over the day, one around nine o'clock when I get up, one at one, and one at five. The Tussionex is just at five, and sometimes at noon if I need it. It lasts for four hours—it's only Afrin that lasts for twelve. Then I take a Dalmane at bedtime, and the day is done.

My friend Deidra's into drugs more than me. She was up for three days straight last week with that singer and her ugly husband smoking crack. She said the girl's toenails were so long they made a clicking sound on her marble terrazzo floor.

Deidra does binges, but I can't afford to do that anymore, not with my career just starting to take off. She's famous enough to do whatever she wants, but I'm not there yet. Deidra's had three careers, TV sitcom to movie star to film director. She just directed her second movie, which Rafael worked on—that's how I met him. He did the sets for her movie about a girl in high school (played by me) who has to have an abortion. Luckily I knew about abortions thanks to my mom and my aunts. Life is funny that way.

A girl in Building A was raped last week with a squeegee pole. As the guards restrained her five female attackers, the girl was seen to be laughing, which was taken as evidence that she liked it. When I overheard two of the officers joking about it in the canteen, I tried to explain just why I thought the girl was laughing, but they looked at me with such contempt that I lost my nerve and hurried away.

Some of the officers are evil by nature. Some are sadists. Others have simply accustomed themselves too well to suffering. It leaves them without empathy, or even interest (one of the definitions of a sociopath). They hate being here. They hate working with women. They would rather have a hundred male prisoners than one woman prisoner. It's the women's voices that get on their nerves, they say.

Many of the guards are former police officers or from the military. Dr. de la Vega told me that half of them will not make it through their first year. That's better than most of the medical staff—we apparently last about three months. I've stopped eating in the canteen.

My cell is in the middle of the tier and it can get pretty noisy. There's nothing to absorb all the sounds, only the steel and the concrete and your own pounding head. The officers' radios are loud, and the sound of their boots. They use those buried-treasure detectors to vacuum in and out of the cells when they look for contraband, and the machines make a beeping sound, even when there's nothing there. Some women wear headphones without music to keep out the noise, but they don't work for me.

The women make even more noise than the officers. Two women yell out their chess moves every night for hours. I don't mind so much cause the words are nice—queens and castles and knights—but someone's been making dog noises for the last few nights, barking and howling till morning, and it's hard to sleep. Whoever wasn't screaming already was screaming at everyone else to SHUT UP.

Every night, the women yell, What time is it? and the guards give the wrong answer just to mess us up. Not that I know the real time, but one guard yells, Nine-thirty-three, and the next one yells, Two-fifteen, so it's not too hard to see they are playing us. It makes me wonder why we can't have our own clocks and watches. Can't do a hang-up with a watch strap. Every night, this one officer shouts back, What the FUCK possible difference could the time make to YOU?

I tried to explain to Dr. Forrest that time here is a little like sound. You can hear it, but you can't see it. I'm not sure she got it.

My analyst doesn't say much, which is as it should be, but now and again he will sigh and say, I am really rather grateful that your mother, shall we say, liked you.

I take this as the deepest confirmation of my sanity, and of hers. I only occasionally wonder if it's true—if, in fact, she did like me. It's hard to know. I was young when she died. My father's nickname for her was Cain 'n' Abel, which passed for wit in San Francisco. She was a sugar heiress from Honolulu, a chilly slender girl who knew that my father had married her for her money. She knew because he told her so on their wedding night. This knowledge did not cause her to leave him or even to dislike him. She simply disappeared into an unusually pleasant life of alcohol, tennis, and docent meetings at the museum to which she'd promised the collection of Asian art she inherited from her own mother. My father had a decorous affair for years with one of his secretaries until my mother's unexpected death made it possible for him to marry her. Divorce, I am sure, was never discussed by my mother and father. It was not a solution available to people like my parents—they were not sophisticated or even very practical. My mother did not behave like a rich woman, which was in the tradition of her missionary ancestors. She didn't appear to want very much of anything. I may be wrong about that. I have no idea what she wanted—that would be a more accurate statement.

. . .

Wanda asked me today if I want to be in their family! If I am familyed, I'll be a daughter. She said what they do is they alienate themselves from everyone else and just have a real good time. The only thing is I'll have to be a little tougher. Which got me worried.

Wanda's brothers taught her how to defend herself when she was a little girl. They used to fight until one of them passed out. Sometimes both of them passed out. She got so she really looked forward to it, and when they started drinking she'd find a comfy spot on the bed to watch. If things weren't going fast enough, she'd jump up and get them more Bacardi. The only thing I ever watched was my brother play with himself, but that was just once, and he didn't know I was watching. It made me feel bad afterward, and I never did it again. I don't think Wanda felt bad about anything ever.

So far Wanda is my one and only friend, but that's my fault. It's always been hard for me to make friends. What I mean is it's hard for me to KEEP friends. It seems once someone gets to know me, that's it. That hasn't been too big a problem here because not many people want to go that first step, but Wanda was nice from day one. She said she wasn't here on this earth to judge me—that was already done in a court of law. I don't need to know any more about that, she said. I felt relieved, but I felt sad, too—a tiny part of me wanted her to know everything. She says most people think I'm here for embezzling cause I'm white and I talk nice. Let's keep it that way, she said. You do for me and I'll do for you. Sure, I said, I'd be happy to.

I had a breakdown when my son Ransom was born, a fact that Rafael later used in our divorce as evidence of my instability. I was in my last year of residency, and I'd been traveling twice a week to Long Island to inject radioactive glucose into men's brains—I was looking for abnormalities in their temporal lobes, and sometimes I found them. I had no idea what I was doing. I'd been trained to believe in pathological models: bad parents make bad people who can be treated with lots of drugs. I saw symptoms and behavior in an a-contextual model. I was not particularly tolerant. I'd like to say that my breakdown was the beginning of my training in compassion, but that would not be the truth. That training has begun only recently.

It was Rafael who decided that the baby would be named Ransom—not in honor of the obscure poet, which is what I thought when I first heard the name, but in reference to the idea that we are all hostages to fortune, a conceit that infuriated me. As I was in a state of manic exultation whenever I managed to wake, a state in which everything was a metaphor, no one paid much attention to my opinion, and the baby was given the name. I could not bring myself to say it for a long time. Which wasn't really a problem at first, since they took him from me the minute he was born, wheeling me straight from the delivery room to the psych ward. I slept for the next two months. I sometimes think that I wasn't crazy at all, just exhausted.

When I was at last allowed to go home, I could not stop crying. I held my baby at arm's length to feed him his bottle of gray soy milk. I wore gloves to bathe him. I had terrifying fantasies that I would hurt him—drop him or drown him or throw him out the window. When Rafael, bored and exasperated, told me that he was going to Hollywood to work on films, I was horrified—it meant that I would be alone with the baby.

I understood that my breakdown had been precipitated, among other swarming things, by the hormonal furor in my brain, but still I was ashamed. I knew that I'd have to find a way to love the child. I'd had a bad start. In the end, I was grateful to be given the chance—I learned to love him through necessity, which is often the case. It may be true of some people that their heart's love is boundless, but I am not made that way. I forced Rafael to marry me and I made him give me a baby, and then I didn't want either of them.

I thought Rafael was from Europe, or some really cool island, when Deidra introduced us that day on the set. He wears those Mexican shirts with the embroidery down the front that don't tuck in, and brown-and-white shoes. Guys in California don't look like Rafael, not even Mexicans. I liked him right away. He told me later I wasn't his type, but that didn't seem to stop him. I saw a picture of his ex-wife, and he wasn't kidding. He met her at a hospital in New York City where she was studying to be a doctor (a part I'd really like to play someday—so far I only get nurses) when he brought in a backup dancer who'd just OD'd on a shoot. They got married five weeks later. Rafael and the doctor. He thought she was rich. He was just starting to get work and he didn't have any money. I don't know what her excuse was. He was surprised to find out when they got divorced that she didn't have as much money as he thought. He once tried to sell some Chinese bowls she got from her mom when she died, and she had a fit. He says she's obsessed with two things—her work and their kid. He would never've ended up living with me if she'd sold her apartment in New York to give him money in the divorce like she was supposed to. He'd been living for two years in a garden apartment behind the Ambassador Hotel when I met him. He spent more money on clothes than rent, I could tell.

He's someone who could help my career, for once. I figure he's probably using me, too, but that's cool. That's how things get done here, and there's nothing wrong with it. Ambition's just another kind of energy. It gives you movement, hopefully up. Besides, he's not some loser to drag me down like my first husband, who, as far as I know, knock on wood, is rotting in some Texas jail. A bunch of Guatemalans he'd hidden in the back of a truck suffocated to death. Typical of him. He never cared about anyone, least of all some poor kids trying to find work.

I decided if Rafael ever finds out about the drugs, I'll tell him I need them for my new teeth. He already knows I'm not good with pain. I have to be put under just for collagen. I had to get rid of Eddie and Mandy when Rafael moved in, which was not easy, believe me. Luckily Deidra had a video of them in bed shooting meth, which helped. I used to spend the night at Deidra's just to get away from them, which is hard to believe, I know, coming from me, but Eddie kept me up all night with his panic attacks, even if he was in Florida when the Towers went down. He said just thinking about his friends burned to a crisp trying to save some accountants made him insane. I was so happy to see Eddie go I cried, which he thought meant I wanted him to stay. Deidra said she never saw anyone stop crying so fast.

She never minds when I show up at her house, even if it's the middle of the night. She likes having people around—people who do drugs tend to like company. Deidra's divorced. She has three assistants, a driver, and a cook. It's not that cool to have a driver in L.A., but Deidra never learned to drive, which she's kind of proud of—it has to do with growing up in New York City. I like to sleep at her house if I have an important audition in the morning. She keeps the temperature so cold I wake up looking really good. Deidra is sixteen years older than me. She's going through an early menopause, or maybe it's just the drugs, and she gets hot flashes. The windows are all locked and the house is set at subzero. I have to sleep in a flannel nightgown and a sweater, but I wake up looking refreshed and not swollen. Everyone's pretty when they're pink and twenty-two, I know, but I wake up really really pink.

I got a letter today from Goren, Sharp, Donnelly and Norbertson, 2080 Avenue of the Stars, Century City, Los Angeles, California, 90067. The letter was registered. The back flap was open, but that's because the guards read it, then check for heroin and LSD. It was a letter from a lawyer, Mr. Gerald M. Sharp, saying if I wrote to his client ever again he would take legal action. I'm not sure what that means. I'm not sure they could really do too much more to me.

What I do know is SHE got my letter. I was really upset when I read his. I could feel my face start to burn. It was just what my mom said would happen. I made a mess of things. That's the last thing I wanted. It was nice of Katie Couric to forward the letter, though.

I met the new head shrink today. She was on the daybook for the hostage talk, and no one wanted to do it, myself included. I can give the hostage talk in my sleep, and probably have. In the end, I traded Lieutenant Sinora for early break and went to see Dr. Louise Forrest.

She had an inmate with her, but the door was closed so I couldn't hear what they were saying. It's pretty funny what you get to hear, the docs not bothering to close their doors, maybe because they think they'll be jumped by one of the girls. It's happened a couple of times. The shrink that used to be here— the one whose place she's taking—had his ear bitten from his head by that lady who shot the judge. I was off that day, but Cready had to find the doc's ear, and apparently it wasn't that easy. Some of the offices are filthy. That happens in prisons. Not that ears are lost that often. I don't want to give the wrong impression.

I waited in the hall, watching her through the glass. The inmate's back was to me, but I would recognize Keesha anywhere. Her head is like a bunch of gray snakes. The doc was facing the door. She's not bad looking. She was wearing a black sweater. I wonder does she know that's against regulations. No tits. Nice neck. A pearl necklace. Also against regulations. She looked up once but pretended not to see me. I was staring pretty hard, trying to read her lips, and I could tell it made her nervous. She was like those girls who act as if they've done something real bad. Then you sneak a look at their records and find out they killed someone in a car by accident one night in a storm or fell asleep while smoking and burned someone's house down. Bad, but not that bad.

Keesha's time was up and I opened the door for her—Hey, Captain Bradshaw, baby, how's my baby?—which finally made the doc look up. She covered her notes with her hands, like I might try to read them upside down, which I did. There was a nice smell in the room—it usually smells of mice up there. She was staring at me, which I'm used to from the docs, only she seemed a little more deliberate about it, like it's a way she's developed with men. Men she maybe likes. She was checking me out, but she didn't want me to know it. Her way of handling it was to act as if our conversation wasn't really that serious, which irritated me. Making herself look cool and me dumb, when in fact she was the one not getting it. I wondered if she was one of those girls who's spent too much time with horses and is just beginning to figure it out, only fifteen years too late. I considered for a minute helping her—it wouldn't have been hard—but something about her bugged me. I thought maybe she was making fun of me. I couldn't be sure. She's a shrink so she's good at hiding what she thinks. Anyway, in the end I just wasn't in the mood. When I left, she reached across the desk and shook my hand.

I never thought I'd be asked to join a family where my mom and dad happen to be two women.

It's a honor Wanda asked me. Sex is forbidden between brothers and sisters, but it's okay for aunts, uncles, cousins, nieces and nephews, and mothers and fathers, of course. Maybe even grandparents, although that seems a little creepy even for them. Brothers and sisters fall in love and have sex, not necessarily in that order, and the incest breaks up the family. At least here it does. They have sex and then they want to start their own family, which messes everything up. You know how we do, Wanda said.

Many of the ladies here wouldn't be gay if they were at home. Being a lesbian is like being in a play for them. It's a performance. Acting gay has saved their lives. Some of them were never loved before, by either man, woman, or child. It's a way to feel safe, despite all the fights. It's also a good way to make time fly. I can see that.

Wanda herself won't be gay once she is outside these walls— I wonder what Jo thinks about that! There is a real shortage of studs here, which means the studs pretty much get the pick of the litter. Where else can a two-hundred-pound woman with boils have all the girls run after her and call her Poppy? They do everything for the studs, bring them things, and braid their hair, just like at home. There is a LOT of jealousy because of it. Last month, someone poured scalding water on Keesha just for passing a new girl a plate of noodles. Wanda says the secret is you got to keep things sectionalized. She is what is called a person with juice. Wanda does not wait in line in the commissary or do her own laundry. She doesn't do anything that someone else could do for her. She doesn't mess with the trash, and she keeps her mind concentrated on doing her time with no trouble. No fluff fluff stuff for Wanda.

She asked if she could borrow some money today. Not much, only thirty dollars, even if that's a lot for here. I don't use it anyway, and it's just sitting in my account. We get money from our families or boyfriends, or girlfriends, too, I suppose, and use it to buy things from the commissary. The food is so starchy the girls like to dress it up with Jo's homemade chili which they buy from Wanda, but that's too hot for me. There is one commissary box just for a sweet tooth. Three kinds of Keebler cookies, including coconut, and all kinds of candy. I'd like that box if I could eat.

Some people send the money they earn here home to their relatives, which comes to about two dollars a day at most, and then they don't have a penny left for theirselves. I feel sorry for them and they're the ones I try to give my mom's boxes to. Shaynna gets money sent to her as death benefits from the gang in Massachusetts her dead husband belonged to. Keesha doesn't have a family to send her things, but she has two outside tricks who write to her. It's easy to get men, especially old ones, to be pen pals. Her ones are crazy about her. They don't know about each other. She keeps their letters tied up in a ribbon, and she'll let you read them if you pay her. She let me read one for free. Everyone thinks they're pretty funny, but I don't.

A Captain Bradshaw came by my office the other day to give me a lesson in hostage taking—I, of course, being the prospective hostage. Captain Bradshaw, I'd been told, is famous for his sigh. He has the look of someone who is an expert on wickedness. He reminds me of the boys I used to admire at soccer camp when I was a girl, although those boys grew up to become captains of industry. His eyes are blue. There is the faintest trace of a scar under his left eye. He's tall, with brown hair combed straight back—he looks more like a German banker than a corrections officer. He does not have a mustache.

I said that I did not know hostage taking was a possibility, and he said, Really? Everything's a possibility.

Afterward, I thought I'd imagined it about the scar. He wrinkles his brow when he wishes to emphasize a point—about the danger of homemade shanks, for example—which gives him a certain appealing sternness. My masochism was stirring. I had a little fantasy, but I got rid of it. I might have held on to it under different circumstances, but I felt that I had a responsibility to concentrate on hostage taking—in the end, an acceptable alternative fantasy.

He said that at the slightest possibility of a riot I was to remove all of my clothing, as well as anything that indicates authority—a badge, a radio with an emergency pull cord, handcuffs, pen, rule book, flashlight, baton, keys, rubber mouthpiece for resuscitation, gloves, money, can of toxic foam, or a pair of shoes. The list made me smile, but then he sighed and I made my face serious. He said that it is essential that I conceal my identity should there be even a hint of inmate unrest. The fact that I am one of the few women not dressed in jeans and a T-shirt would be something of a giveaway, I said, and he said, That's why you take your clothes off, doctor. They really get caught up in the situation they get caught up in.

What I did not tell Captain Bradshaw, out of vanity as well as a desire that he like me, is that I would never take off my clothes. All the same, I was grateful for my lesson. I hope that there will be more. It gives me an illusion of safety. Surely a semblance of power is better than no power at all. I think Captain Bradshaw may have been flirting with me. It's been so long, I couldn't be sure. I lost interest in that sort of thing when Ransom was born. Still, it gave a lift to the day.

I've been a little down, but Wanda brought me more magazines tonight after her work detail, and that cheered me right up. I'd already read them, but I didn't tell her that. It was her visit that made me feel good.

Wanda will be here for a hundred and twenty more months. I don't know what I'll do when she's gone. Her husband and one of her kids was killed in a car she was driving when she was high on drugs, which at least is manslaughter and not a capital crime. She was a nurse's aide before she came here. That's how she knows so much about drugs. She says prison is what she always imagined college would be. It's the only time in her life anyone was nice to her. Before coming here, she was in the desert near Tucson. At night she'd listen to the snakes slither across the cement floor of her cell and the squeaks of the rats as the snakes grabbed them and ate them.

The women from the same town and even the same state stick together no matter what and share what they have, though the women from L.A. hate the women from New York, and the women from New York hate the women from L.A. Wanda, who is a *reina* in the Latin Queens, says it's because of gangs. She really is a queen. She has black and gold beads from her gang in the Bronx. The prisons out west are clean, she says—maybe the snakes keep them clean—but the prisons in New York are mean. Also the men guards are a hundred times more relaxed here. Some female guards make extra money by being prostitutes to prisoners, but they can't do that at Sloatsburg. The inmates do it theirselves. Tammy G. in Number 45 had to go to the infirmary with a sexually transmitted disease, and you know what that means. They found out when she swallowed a broken lightbulb. Officer Huff from the weekend shift gave her the infection. Officer Huff is married to a former inmate, which is funny considering the guards aren't supposed to have anything to do with us. They're not even supposed to know who's a terrorist and who just wrote a bad check. That's so we'll all be treated the same, even if it doesn't really work that way.

Wanda says Captain Bradshaw used to be a undercover cop, but he got shot and retired. Just look at the man's ears, she said. He has four little holes on one earlobe, which had been for his undercover earrings. All the girls who aren't gay are in love with him, and even some of the ones who are. I can see why, and it's not just cause he's cute.

Reading through the maternal filicide records of the city of Chicago, I discovered that there were no convictions of women for murdering their children between 1870 and 1930. For sixty years, the women were hospitalized, treated, and released.

None of them ever committed another murder. Any mother who killed her child was, by the very nature of her crime, out of her mind and needed treatment, not punishment. The public was more forgiving of these women than they are now.

Most state laws require two conditions for a jury to return a sentence of death: the defendant must be considered a danger to society, and no mitigating factors may warrant the lesser sentence of life imprisonment. Insanity is not considered a mitigating factor. An IQ of fifty is not a mitigating factor, nor is a childhood of torture and abuse. The standard police manual on interrogation and confessions says that the mentally handicapped have a special susceptibility to questioning and a willingness to admit to crimes that they did not in fact commit, but a mental handicap is not a mitigating factor. Neither is postpartum psychosis. If I really had thrown Ransom out the window, I might be dead now.

Deidra teases me because of my little tweaks and phobias, for instance having to shave my legs every day, rain or shine, no matter where I am. I once tried the side of a scissors when I'd run out of my special razors on location (the production assistant fired for that one) and the nearest drugstore was seventy miles away across Death Valley. I had the razors in the morning, though. I myself do not find that a particularly weird phobia, given some of the people I know and what they do to themselves and others. It doesn't involve anyone but myself (the assistant doesn't count, she was stealing from me anyway), and if it doesn't hurt anyone, I don't see what's wrong with it. I explained to Deidra I can't sleep at night unless I just shaved my legs. I want her to tell me about her phobias, but she says she doesn't have any. That, I can tell you, I do not believe. I'll get them out of her eventually. She treats me like a kid sister. I once asked her if she had sisters of her own, and she said, Oh, yeah, but I could tell she didn't want to talk about it.

We are required to give tests to certain of the new inmates, and lately I have insisted on giving the exams myself so as to ensure the outcome. A prisoner may be sent here for ninety days while a judge takes his time to determine whether she deserves a harder sentence or she can safely be sent to rehabilitation or a halfway house. That is where I come in. I do everything in my power to get her released into rehab.

The women sent for observation have stolen a lipstick, or carried a bag of marijuana for a boyfriend, or bought a microwave they knew was stolen. The purpose of the ninety-day sentence is to scare them so profoundly that they will never again drive while under the influence of alcohol or leave Saks Fifth Avenue with a cashmere sweater in their underpants.

They fall apart the minute they're locked up. The intricate etiquette of prison behavior is unknown to them. The other inmates will not speak to them. They are unaware how to obtain the simplest things—a bar of soap, toilet paper, sanitary napkins, prescription medicine. If they are taking medication for depression or diabetes or epilepsy, and are without their pills when they are arrested, they go into withdrawal. The women with serious drug addictions are more fortunate—they're thrown into solitary and given methadone for five days.

Jo got caught cooking in her cell last night when the smell of garlic went all down the tier, but she got only a inmate misbehavior report. She uses one of those little black coils from a kitchen stove with two wires attached to a plug, and they said she could set the place on fire or burn someone with it. Wanda said she could also fucking short-circuit the breakers if she fucking felt like it, but she never fucking did, and didn't that tell you something. The officer who wrote her up is new and that's why. No one ever bothered about it before.

There was a big fuss tonight when the new girl in Number 49 ate the soles of her sneakers and almost died. I was standing at my usual place by the door and heard everything. They will swallow anything here! Last week, a girl got in a fight with her boyfriend on the phone and she took a paper clip and ripped open a scar on her stomach where she had a baby a month ago. There was blood all over the place. It made me feel bad for her. Not the fight so much, but about her baby. Where is that baby now, I'd like to know.

Dr. Fischl has made me—just for fun, he says, his beard twitching—a laminated card which states that I am Unfit to Render an Opinion on Anything Because of Sympathy for Criminals.

It's true that I'm partial. I try to disguise it, but clearly I am not succeeding. When I first came here, I was agitated all the time, desperate to resolve my loyalties—who was good, who was bad, and, even more trying for me, whether it mattered. This is a particularly dangerous thing for a physician (I caution myself against the obvious), but I've learned a little since then. It has been only eight months since I came here—it seems like ten years. I'm still agitated, but my loyalties, at least, are a little less confused.

I could tell Dr. Forrest thought it was weird it took me so long to find a name for Shane. When Shane was born, I was pretty messed up about it. Which means, if I am being as honest as I can, I didn't know what to do with his penis. How to clean him, or how to touch him. How to LOOK at him even. He was so strange to me! I was more comfortable with Kaley, even though I was shocked when I washed her in the beginning and found some white stuff in her tiny vagina—it was like a little secret pouch. I was shocked because I thought only grown-up women had that, like I thought only men played with theirselves and only women went to psychiatrists. I learned better when I was in Marcy Hospital, on all counts, but that was later. I was always pretty dumb about sex, which is funny when you think about what I did.

I used to think about his testicles a lot. They were like little red grapes and they made me shudder if I touched them by accident. Sometimes I couldn't wash him, and days would go by until my mom would have to come over and give him a bath in the sink. I learned to do it, like I learned to love him, and when I did, I couldn't love him or wash him enough. He was the cleanest baby in Huntington, Long Island.

It's difficult for me when Ransom goes to California to see his father. I was so relieved when he returned last month that I couldn't stop talking. It wasn't until I saw the alarm in his eight-year-old eyes that I became aware of my incipient mania and forced myself to slow down. The minute he went to school, I ransacked his backpack as if he were a lover I suspected of betrayal. Which, of course, he was. Oh, I know his father loves him and desires his happiness and health, but I am the one who really loves him. No one can love him the way that I love him. And no one else can be loved quite so much in return, either.

Rafael's girlfriend is an actress. I've been reading about her. I found some of Helen's magazines and brought them home with me. She's nominated for a Golden Globe for her performance in a movie about teenaged girls in the sixties. I asked my friend Miranda, who works for a talent agency in Beverly Hills, if she knew anything about her, and she described her in a misperceived attempt to make me feel better as one of those actresses who likes to date grips. That is like having sexual relations with the pool man or the roofing contractor. It isn't a practice that translates particularly well to New York—it's not quite the same as having an affair with the super.

I'm ashamed to say that I asked Ransom about her. I couldn't help myself. What is Angie like with Daddy? Do they go to bed early? Order Chinese food? To his credit, he was not a cooperative witness. All he said is that you do not order take-out food in Los Angeles. It irritated me and made me think him disloyal. My feelings were hurt, which was, of course, my intention. Only when he said that he had no bedtime in California, could watch television all day long, and drink soda at midnight did I begin to wonder if he was trying to provoke me. I think Angie must be a nice person, I said. He glanced at me to see if I was setting a trap, but when he saw that I meant it, he smiled in gratitude. She's pretty cool, he said shyly. Then, warming to his subject: We go to the beach, and sometimes we steal things.

I did not press him further.

I was standing by the door of my cell tonight—I didn't turn on my light and it looked like Halloween with the orange glow on the walls—when two guards started talking at the duty officer's desk. I couldn't see them, but I think I recognized their voices. One of them said, I finally met the new doc. His voice was low and cool. Was she wearing those black boots? the other voice said. I couldn't see all of her, said the first voice. She was at her desk. She seems a little full of herself, said the second voice. I looked up her employment records, said the first voice. She's new at this. Let's see how long her nerves hold out, said the second voice.

They walked down the gallery, laughing. I stood there till my teeth began to chatter, and then I got back into bed.

I have a patient named Jessie in Building D who is serving fifteen years for third-degree murder, aggravated assault, unauthorized practice of medicine, and animal cruelty—at the time of her arrest, a dead dachshund was found hanging from the back porch of her mobile home.

Jessie castrated herself when she was seventeen. Her fifth husband recently cut off his own genitals after discovering that they were in love with the same woman. Jessie performed emergency surgery on him, strapping him to an ironing board and sewing on his balls with a needle and poultry thread. Although he bled profusely over the next few days, an autopsy revealed that he died from an overdose of prescription painkillers.

Despite her neutered state, Jessie feels that she belongs in a men's prison. She's convinced that she would be happier there, and I agree with her. I've requested a transfer on her behalf. Unlike my former husband, I'm not interested in kitsch. I don't think Jessie's predicament is a metaphor. I also don't think she'll be transferred.

Aida didn't show up for group today (Friday at noon). I learned later from Dr. Henska that Aida has been sent to intensive management lockup for burning another inmate with the stinger she uses to heat food. (No more egg fuck young, said Dr. Henska.) Aida, possessed of a greater intensity than most people care to tolerate, attacks with admirable fury anyone who is misguided enough to tease her. She's been in detention so many times that the maximum-security guards are always delighted to see her and greet her with affection, even though it was Aida who made a formal complaint last summer that the officers were watching her shower with what Aida considered excessive interest, resulting in a change in the way the inmates bathe (transparent shower curtains). Aida's was an unusual victory, as women do not customarily file complaints or suits. Dr. de la Vega, who, it turns out, has a law degree in addition to his medical degree, tells me that very few changes in state or federal law have been instigated by female prisoners.

A little Dexedrine, a platinum AmEx, and voilà you get speed shopping, one of my most favorite things in the world. No matter how rich I will be, I will never beat Deidra's record, which is ten thousand dollars in four different shops in Beverly Hills in a little less than three hours for a grand total of forty-three thousand dollars, which is pretty impressive even if she had her driver Mohammed return most of the stuff the next day. It's amazing the salesgirls go along with it when they know it's coming back anyway. No one ever says, not even the manager, Hey, babe, you don't even fit that three-thousand-dollar sweater! They've been through it lots of times, but each time they're so excited and nice you'd think it was real. It is real, Deidra says. It's like they're high, too, only it's on movie stars, not speed. Deidra has a way with the common people, as she likes to say, but that's because she's from Bensonhurst in New York, which anyone can tell the minute she opens her mouth. I know how many hours she spent with a special speech therapist (nine) before she said fuck it and just turned it into this asset and right off got that TV series about court stenographers.

I'd seen her two or three times, and we have the same colorist, but we'd never really met. I once spotted her in the waiting room at Dr. Miller's, where I listened in on a conversation she was having. I was picking things up as fast as I could—let's just say I had plenty of time to make up for. She pointed to one side of her nose and said, Ten thousand, and then to the other side, Ten thousand, and then to the tip, Five thousand. Which made me rethink everything. I liked her right away.

Helen spoke for the first time today about her son. I knew, of course, that he was autistic because I have her records. She said that she'd tried to teach him at home, but she eventually had to send him to school when he became too difficult for her. You could not say the number three in his presence, and he went into a frenzy at the sight of the color red. He didn't like school. He couldn't tell what was a game and what wasn't, so he turned everything into a contest—the first to finish snack, the first to put on his coat—causing the other children to despise him. Even the teachers disliked him. Helen is convinced that one of them wore a red scarf just to torment him. Once his homeroom teacher made him clean it up when another boy blew his nose on him. He had calluses on his legs from sliding back and forth in his chair and was prescribed high dosages of Ritalin. He used to hide behind a shed in the schoolyard so as not to return to the classroom after recess, wandering around the cold yard for hours until a teacher finally brought him inside. Eventually, the school refused to take him.

．．．

I can't believe it, but I got a letter from her! I am so happy. She was very nice in the letter. She wants to keep it a secret just between us. She says, Yes, we are sisters! Even though that is not what I meant, I understand what she means. I am honored to just be her friend. She gave me her private address.

I wonder if she knows they read our mail. It's not like they'll report us to Mr. Gerald Sharp, but you can't be too careful, as she herself says. She sent me a autographed picture, but without my name on it, which was a little disappointing. I want to make something for her. A sweater in pink and purple. Colors of the sunset to go with her golden hair.

First a letter, and now I'm allowed out of my cell. I can go to the machine for my own Sno-Caps. I can go to the library. I can buy stamps. This has been a wonderful week.

My nerves are bad. If I were treating myself, which I'm not, I'd say I was depressed. I've been dreaming about my patient Helen. She told me that she dreams about me, too.

I've increased my dosage of Wellbutrin another hundred milligrams. More than two drinks a day renders the benefits of the drug fairly useless, so it is a bit of a compromise. I am so distracted that I often dress myself by putting on a sock before pulling on one pant leg of my trousers. Then perhaps my brassiere. Sometimes one shoe before the brassiere. The increase in dosage makes my hands shake.

I met one of the new ladies yesterday waiting for my meds. Her name is Shirley. She told me right off she is here because her twelve-year-old son hung himself while she was at a Mary Kay party. That isn't what she was convicted for, though. She was locked up because her house is a pigsty. Two years for being a bad housekeeper! Her son was tortured at school by the other kids, and the teachers just looked the other way. He wore glasses. He smelled because Shirley wouldn't wash his clothes. She's appealing her sentence.

Keesha gave me a picture tonight of Shirley's son. She tore it out of a newspaper cause she knows I'm interested in that kind of thing. Dr. Forrest says there are lots of women in prison who have killed one or more of their kids. There are sixty-eight in one prison in Texas alone. I had no idea, and no one else does, either. I was pretty shocked. It's just not always in the papers and on TV. I wonder how many is more than one.

Women in here make up stories, but I am telling the truth— I always kept my children clean.

I see LizAnn for an hour every Tuesday morning in private session. She is a small delicate redhead with freckles who will be in prison for two more years if she isn't granted parole at her hearing in May. She has been here for almost three years. As a seventeen-year-old schoolgirl, she kept her newborn premature son in her closet, feeding him before she went to school each morning and when she returned in the evening from soccer practice. Her younger sister found the baby while looking for a sticker album—she said on the *Sally Jessy Raphael Show* that she thought it was really cool to have your own E.T. The baby was too weak to cry. Many hidden babies are suffocated accidentally when the mother panics and tries to muffle its cries, but LizAnn's baby died when an ice skate fell on it. She says it struck him like a sledgehammer in the heart.

LizAnn had no intention of killing her child. She was so heavily medicated during her trial, even though the examining psychiatrist rightly found no evidence of insanity, that she slept through it. (Amy Grossberg, the teenager who left her newborn son in a Dumpster, was sentenced to thirty months in prison, and the father, her fellow student, was sentenced to twenty-four months.) LizAnn is taking a correspondence course to become a veterinary assistant. She collects plastic forks from the commissary trash to send to a Little Sisters of the Poor orphanage in Nicaragua. I've been giving her books. She just finished *Wuthering Heights* and is now reading *Jane Eyre*. Darla says that LizAnn is under the special protection of Captain Bradshaw. Whatever that means.

Officer Cready's Tip for February: You got six hundred thousand female inmates let out each year, and three hundred thousand of them come back. What does that tell you?

. . .

I saw Captain Bradshaw today on my way to administration. We nodded at each other. Later I went to the basement to look for a file. The employment files are kept there, too. It seems that Captain Bradshaw is a former New York City police officer and undercover narcotics detective. He worked for fifteen years in Brooklyn. He has many citations for bravery. He retired early due to an injury—an accidental gunshot wound. His first name is Henry, but he is called Ike. He is married to a nurse who works for Homeland Security. They have one child, a daughter. He lives in Yonkers. He is thirty-seven years old. It sounds like a TV show.

Just before Rafael left for Hollywood—he said he'd be back in a month—he gave me a brown plastic vibrator. It looked like a hot dog, which may be why he named it Oscar. At least, I assume that is why. He hoped that it would remind me of him— I thought him a bit presumptuous, but I said nothing. Thank you, I said. It was returned to its box the minute that he left for the airport, and slipped under the bed. I took Rafael's present from its box tonight. The batteries were dead, but I used it anyway. I kept thinking, If Rafael could see me now. Could see us now.

Last night, Wanda asked me to pin for her and Jo, and I was proud to do it. It wasn't the first time, either. Just because I'm not into that kind of thing doesn't mean I won't help a friend in need. It upset me in the beginning even if it was just someone holding hands, but I'm better now. All I had to do last night was keep Officer Molina busy for as long as I could, which isn't that hard for me. Once I get started, I jump all over the place and lose track of what I'm saying, like a crazy person. Sometimes I even have to stop and ask, Where am I?

Officer Molina listened for as long as he could take it and when I saw his mind start to wander—I thought at first he'd fallen asleep—I began to sing as loud as I could, which was the signal he'd be coming their way. He's been here a long time so he didn't think it was strange when I suddenly started shouting the song from *The Little Mermaid*, only nodded his head and walked away. Later Jo said, Thank you, mi amor, for keeping Officer Molina so long, and I felt happy I could help out.

In a recent e-mail, my former husband suggests that I take Dr. Melfi of *The Sopranos* as a model, as she, too, works with psychopaths. It seems that Dr. Melfi, a most satisfied user of the drug Zoloft, has become a spokesman for Pfizer, the pharmaceutical company that makes Zoloft, and Rafael wonders if I might obtain a similar endorsement. Perhaps Rafael thinks Dr. Melfi is a real doctor.

I'm tempted now and then to tell Rafael that he is wrong about me. I do have ambition. I've always known what I wanted. I wanted a child, for example, and he helped me to get one. Sometimes, although not often, I wonder what he wants. He claims that he was able to move from production assistant to production designer in no time at all because African Americans like him, which is probably true. I know that he believes in beauty (or at least style) and its concomitant rewards, not unlike the way that I believe in the unconscious. I find his sense of taste forbidding, and I know he would say the same of my theories.

He sent me an article today from the archives of the *New York Daily News:* "First I stripped her naked. How she did kick, bite and scratch. I choked her to death, then cut her in small pieces so I could take my meat to my rooms. How sweet and tender her little ass was roasted in the oven. It took me nine days to eat her entire body. I did not fuck her tho I could have had I wished. She died a virgin." Rafael wrote that the murderer, a Mr. Fish, was executed in 1938, an addendum for which I found myself grateful.

He also forwarded me an e-mail from his girlfriend's psychic on Maui, in which I was less interested. The psychic has rather precise views as to my career path. She is worried about me. That my former husband would give the date of my birth to some con artist infuriates me, and I consider this sharing of my vitals, as he puts it, an invasion of privacy. I really do prefer to organize my own hopes and failures, and I don't intend to be deprived of that pleasure.

I was irritated by the psychic's mumbo jumbo. I hate the idea that someone is thinking presciently about me. People have a similar view of psychiatry. I wonder, Did Rafael tell the psychic that she and I have a life's work in common? I'm sure she earns more money than I do. She said that my planets were in a suitable alignment for both love and mayhem. With any luck, they'll arrive at the same time. The only thing I miss about Rafael is his pale brown cock.

. . .

A box from the commissary came today, a present from my mom. It has two extra-sharp-Cheddar squeeze cheeses, powdered eggs, beef jerky, four packs of strawberry Hubba Bubba, and three bags of Goya oregano, garlic salt, and dried pimentos. It's crazy my mother sends me spicy things. She must of forgot she used to make me chew jalapeños when she said I made things up. Sometimes I had to eat so many I had blisters all over my face. One pepper for every lie. Sometimes I couldn't swallow for days. She told my favorite teacher I was a natural-born liar. I never got over that.

I saw Captain Bradshaw today outside the Visit Room. He was escorting Jessie, the transsexual. Jessie had hold of his hand, which Bradshaw didn't seem to mind. Jessie was wearing eye makeup and lipstick, I noticed, which I thought was against the rules. Bradshaw tipped his hat to me in what may or may not have been an ironic gesture. I was so awkward that I couldn't think of a thing to say. It seemed to amuse him. I've never been very good about men. I even prefer my patients to be women, which is fortunate given my place of work, although hardly an accident. Jessie would know how to talk to Bradshaw. In fact, she *was* talking to him. Maybe I should take lessons.

I was reading Freud tonight when I couldn't sleep—it does the trick when everything else has failed. It's a habit I learned from Professor Cluff, a man of such magnificent weirdness that I was in love with him for years. He was the first man with whom I had an orgasm, even if he believed, all five times, that it originated in the vagina.

This quote is from *Three Essays on the Theory of Sexuality:* "When at last the sexual act is permitted and the clitoris itself becomes excited, it still retains a function: the task, namely, of transmitting the excitation to the adjacent female sexual parts, just as—to use a simile—pine shavings can be kindled in order to set a log of harder wood on fire."

If Ellie confided in me all the things she saw, my heart would burst. When my bottom would bleed and my underpants got stained, my mother would make me take medicine for worms, even though I TOLD her it wasn't from that. Later, I must of got used to it, the way you do, cause the bleeding stopped, though when I was pregnant with Shane the doctor wanted to know where all the scars came from. I said I didn't know, and he never mentioned it again. Jimmy never noticed them. I used to think it was a good thing Jimmy was the only person I ever slept with (not a relation) cause I would of been too ashamed with anyone else of how messed up I was down there. The thing about Uncle Dad is once I got my period, he stopped putting his penis inside me, at least in front, so he wouldn't get me pregnant. His hand, yes, and other things, but mostly he used my bottom. He didn't want to get in trouble.

My mom doesn't remember about the worms. I asked her about it once. Even my brother Kelly doesn't remember, which might make me think I imagined it, except Kelly's not the most reliable. He's doing another tour in Iraq now. He was prosecuted last year for damaging U.S. property when he shot himself in the toe so he wouldn't have to go back. He spent three months in the brig and then they sent him right back to Baghdad.

I found a letter in Helen's file that her husband, James Nash, wrote on her behalf during the sentencing period of her trial: "In conclusion, Your Honor, Ladies and Gentlemen of the Jury, Learned Representatives of the Legal Profession, Esteemed Members of the World Press and Television—I would like you to consider some important issues which didn't have their chance to come up at Mrs. Nash's trial, issues which just might have brought you all to another decision. I respectfully ask for your understanding and consideration to please let my wife live. She tragically stepped into a living hell the day her daughter was born and within twenty-five months she lost her mind. But given the chance to bring in the many religious healers I've had waiting—I will show you that she never lost her soul, only her brain!!! There have already been two tragic deaths, don't let it be three."

After the sentencing, Mr. Nash appeared on many talk shows to celebrate his wife's escape from the electric chair and gave numerous interviews, occasions when he took the opportunity to read this letter aloud. In addition to his job at a computer store and his church work, Mr. Nash is a volunteer with a new group called the Parents of Victims of Ungodly Crimes.

. . .

D r. Forrest talks like a book sometimes. She said it was cold and foggy today, the mist rising from the marshes. I asked her, Were we near a river? and she looked surprised. I explained that when they brought me here it was the middle of the night, and I wasn't in very good shape. Yes, she said after a while, we're near a river. Sometimes you can smell it. Then she said she wished I could see the water and the sky!

Sometimes I pretend I agree with her, especially when she talks about Ellie. I have apologized to Ellie a thousand times, a MILLION times for what I made her go through. I KNOW how she suffered. Sometimes she would take it out on me in little ways, but I always deserved it. I never blamed her, even if it made her secretly happy when I hurt myself. She'd ride on the back of my bike to help me look for pieces of glass in the street or tin cans and other sharp things. Sometimes she'd fight about going to Uncle Dad, even when she knew I'd rather die than see his ugly face again. Still, if Ellie hadn't done what she did all those years, I don't know what would of happened to me. That probably sounds like a funny thing to say, seeing as what happened to me is I am sitting in prison for the rest of my natural life. Who knows, it could of been worse. How is that, you might ask. And to tell the truth, I don't have a answer for that. I don't mean that I could be dead. That would NOT be worse. Sometimes I wonder what my unnatural life would be.

T he docs tend not to talk much to the guards, but I've developed an unlikely relationship with Officer M. Rossi, who works in Building C. She sometimes accompanies me on my psychiatric rounds just for, in her words, the heck of it. Officer Rossi, who is a born-again Christian, is said to have a chronically stiff neck from thirty years of looking the other way. She says, They'll talk you to death, doc, if you let them. Don't ever forget, you're their TV. They have nothing to do all day but sit around and try to get you to do what they want.

She is always neatly dressed in tight gray trousers with sharp creases, a white shirt with short sleeves, and a maroon tie. She wears quite a bit of scent—it smells like pesticide. Calvin Klein, I'd say. A coffee mug with the logo of the Bureau of Prisons is attached by a metal clip to one of her belt loops, alongside a chain with forty square-shaped keys. She's been here so long that some of the women shout after her, Hey Rossi! My grand-moms says hi!

She prefers working with incarcerated men because they know how to take no for an answer (not something I've found to be particularly true). She is contemptuous of all but the most vicious criminals. Ask any prison administrator in the country, in the whole world, she says, and he'll tell you every darn time: Give me a nice murderer any day.

I'm afraid that I've already been fooled a number of times by the inmates, but I don't admit that to Officer Rossi. I haven't yet slipped anyone a gun or even an aspirin. Ms. Morton was recently given a warning for bringing Helen a subscription form to a needlework magazine. Officer Rossi told me not to feel too bad for Morton. The reprimand would have been the same had she inflicted bodily injury on an inmate or come to work drunk. It's in the rule book, she said. That's all. They've got to give you a warning, but it doesn't mean a thing.

. . .

I got another letter from that lady in prison. It didn't take as long to get here this time, now that she has my address. I'm not a very trustful person, but I actually believe her when she says she doesn't want anything. She did ask for another photograph, this one signed to her, but that I cannot do. No evidence, thank you very much. At least she didn't ask for a car. I guess being locked up limits what you can ask for.

She wants to know if I have kids. She wants to know what it was like when I was growing up, and about my mom and dad. Basically, she wants to know did I have a happy childhood. It's funny, but she got me thinking. To tell the truth, I don't have too many memories, good or bad, from before I was fifteen. I ran away a couple of times, and I got as far as Raleigh once, but that's about it in the memory department. I remember cause my dad sent the Marines after me. Really. He was in the service.

Not remembering could be a serious problem when it comes to my acting technique and I need to go deep, but I've learned to just fake it, which I figure is the same thing. Deidra makes up dreams when she goes to her therapist. Sometimes we make up dreams together in bed, and it can get pretty wild. What's hard is to remember them in the morning. I told the lady in prison I had one kid.

My private sessions with Darla are illuminating, if disturbing. She is brought to my office every Wednesday at three o'clock by her escort guard. She sits across from me in one of the metal chairs. I give her a gray blanket from the file cabinet, and she flings it around her shoulders like a shawl. She often remarks on what I'm wearing—not always approvingly—and she's usually right. She told me last week that my boots did not go with my skirt.

She said today that when she was at Chowchilla in California the male inmates regularly gave the guards drugs and money to let them inside the women's cells. She was raped twice by convicts who entered her cell when she was asleep. There is that about Darla, despite her psychosis, that leads me to believe her. I can see that her beauty makes all human, as well as intergalactic, exchanges complicated for her. It is not a problem that I've ever had. I have other things, I know, and I am grateful for them—my discipline and my objectivity and my intelligence—but it would have been nice to have that other thing, too. Even with the complications.

When Darla is not corresponding with her boyfriend, who is in Sing Sing without chance of parole, she paints greeting cards with personalized messages for the other inmates. She showed me the card she designed for Aida's young daughter, whose seventh birthday is next month. She's good—it was an ink drawing of Red Riding Hood and a very pleased wolf skipping hand in hand through the woods.

It's raining tonight. You might wonder how I could know that! It's because the guards coming on the night shift all have wet hair.

It's funny, but one reason I don't like to think about things is it makes me want to do stuff to myself. Like now. Good things and bad things. That's how I got the cuts on my arms. Good things would be how Ellie calms me down. Sometimes she will use her fingers, which is what I like best. I can't find her tonight and now I'll have to do it myself. Last night, I was bleeding which maybe is what brought all this back to me.

In the session today, Keesha, who has served nine sentences since she arrived from Jamaica twenty years ago, all of them for possession of drugs and prostitution, said that the best thing she ever did for her son was to get herself arrested when she was five months pregnant. It was the only way she knew to have a healthy pregnancy. She'd been in prison so many times it didn't frighten her. The streets frightened her. She deliberately approached an undercover police officer, but the officer, who knew her from past arrests and the occasional on-the-house blow job, didn't want to arrest her. In anticipation of this, she had two grams of cocaine in her purse. I was cool to be inside, she said, cause I knew my baby would be taken care of. Clean blankets, real baby clothes, formula—compared to my outside life, it was a goddamn spa. Once he got himself born, it was up to him. I never saw him again. He's about eight years old now.

Shaynna said that her grandmother is so attached to Shaynna's young daughter that she has a fit each time Shaynna is released from prison. The last time, her grandmother hid the child for a month—Shaynna is barred from her grandmother's apartment, as felons are not allowed to live in certain public housing. Her grandmother had Shaynna and her two sisters working as prostitutes in the Bronx when they were nine years old. Shaynna's mother was in Kirby Forensic at the time, a maximum-security hospital on Wards Island where Shaynna and her sisters visited her once a year in their Halloween costumes. It's not so bad there, Shaynna says—it's coed and they have bingo nights. Shaynna's grandmother, who is fifty-one years old (sixteen years older than I am), also looks after Shaynna's sisters' four children, who are between the ages of three and six. Shaynna pronounces the word kid as keed, so it sounds as if she is speaking not of a human child but of some rare creature.

Keesha wanted to know if Shaynna's grandmother had put Shaynna's five-year-old daughter on the street yet. Shaynna began to cry. A good mother is one who knows when to give up her kid, she said. You knew your son was better off without you. Because drugs will always win. Drugs is stronger than kids. A bad mother wants to keep her kids even if she can't take care of them. You were a good mother, she said to Keesha, wiping the tears from her face. You'll get him back someday.

I don't want him back, said Keesha.

I stopped by Forrest's office today to let her know that LizAnn has earned enough privileges to be given a Labrador to train for the blind. The dogs are kept in their own cells behind Building B, tended by a retired alcoholic corrections officer named O'Shaughnessy who happens to be my wife's uncle. The dogs are hurried under guard to the prison each morning as if they might attempt a jailbreak. I like to stand at the east port and watch them. I swear some of them smile.

A lot of the inmates who volunteer to train dogs never had an animal before. Larissa had an episode last month when the dog she'd had for a year was taken back. Larissa, locked up for shoplifting a lawn mower (a repeat offense), understood she'd have the dog for only a year, but she couldn't let him go when the year was up. Everyone was upset, even Rossi. Larissa was sedated and the dog dragged from the prison. I know about it from Officer Molina. I thought at first he was sorry for Larissa, but he was talking about the dog. Molina thinks prison's a shitty place for a dog.

I didn't have to let Forrest know—I could have done it by memo, or not done it at all, it not being required to notify the docs of privilege counts. But Cready had bet me fifty bucks I couldn't get her to the Annex. As I was leaving her office, I asked if she wanted to get a drink after work. It was that simple. I don't know what was bugging Cready.

She was waiting in front when I came out from changing my clothes. It was windy and her hair was blowing in her face. She took a knit cap from her bag and put it on, and we walked across the parking lot. Cready was already at the bar when we got there—his eyes popped out when he saw I actually had her with me. And then he told her my life story. The only thing he left out was the time I got shot, but that was out of professional pride. Believe me, he'd be happy to make me look bad, but cops getting shot is a whole other category. Especially when the shooter is your own wife. He even brought up the basketball championship. I thought he'd never shut up. I've never heard him talk so much. No one could get a word in edgewise, even if they'd wanted to.

She seemed like she was interested, but you couldn't really tell, and finally she said she had to leave. I was surprised she lasted that long. For a minute, I thought he was going to insist on driving her to Manhattan, but he got hold of himself. It took me a while to figure it out. He likes her. Cready likes the doc! Maybe she's a relief after five hundred screaming women. Cready's married. He should know better. There is something about her, I admit. Her hands were shaking, I noticed.

She didn't want anyone to walk her to the train station. It seemed important to her. She said she didn't want to take us away from the basketball game on TV, and I wondered for a minute if she was putting us on. In the end, it was easier just to let her do what she wanted. Being around women whose opinions and feelings don't count for anything makes you lazy. Still, I won the bet.

I went out for a drink after work with H. Bradshaw and P. Cready—no first names, please, only an initial on the name tag to maintain a pretense of anonymity. I'm afraid that I was a little overexcited. I think Bradshaw noticed, but he behaved as if we went out for drinks every night, and it helped—at least I stopped trembling. I was elated in a way that made me feel shy. A little like going to a bar for the first time, fake ID in hand—not that I ever went to bars. I was too busy doing my homework.

I waited for him while he changed into his street clothes, and then we walked to a bar a few blocks from the prison called the Annex that is frequented by policemen, nurses, flight attendants, and corrections officers. I didn't see any psychiatrists. You might wonder how I knew that, since no one was in his work clothes, but I can identify a psychiatrist at fifty yards.

Officer Cready was at the bar when we arrived. He was drinking Guinness. Captain Bradshaw ordered a gimlet. I ordered a vodka and tonic and put a twenty-dollar bill on the bar. I saw Bradshaw look at it, and I wondered if he was going to hand it back to me, but he didn't. Cready held his glass with his little finger extended. I read the other day that a man's ring finger should be longer than his index finger. It is considered a commendable sign of aggression. I noticed that Bradshaw's two fingers were exactly the same length. My ring finger is longer than my index finger, the way a man's is meant to be, but it does not signify in a woman. I couldn't see the length of Cready's fingers, as he was wearing tan leather driving gloves.

Captain Bradshaw and Officer Cready both graduated from St. Ignatius College in Poughkeepsie, although Cready is a year older than Bradshaw. Bradshaw was captain of the basketball team—Cready told me this immediately. He never stopped talking. He teased Bradshaw about his wife, who works at the Immigration Detention Center at Kennedy Airport. She examines suspicious-looking travelers lest they be carrying the Black Death. These people have the oddest jobs.

Although Captain Bradshaw was not on duty, he wore a gun in a shoulder holster in case he bumped into a former prisoner. No one is allowed to carry a gun inside the prison, of course—our motto is Gloves, Cuffs, and Attitude. When he saw me staring at it, he said that even an inmate you've had a friendly relationship with for years can snap and suddenly drive a ballpoint pen through your throat. Just like marriage, said Officer Cready.

There was a basketball game on the television above the bar, and their eyes kept drifting to it. They couldn't help it. It was not the first time I've regretted not having brothers. When I said that I had to leave, they seemed embarrassed. You didn't finish your drink, Cready said, somewhat shocked. He said he'd walk with me the few blocks to the train station, but I said I preferred to go alone. Bradshaw stared at me and then, after a moment, returned his gaze to the television, giving Cready a funny look on the way.

I waited forty minutes on the dark platform, shivering with cold and cursing myself for running away. When I finally reached home, Evelyn was sitting on a chair in the dark kitchen in her coat, her handbag in her lap. Ransom, she said, had been asleep for hours. As it was only nine o'clock, I thought it unlikely, but she is allowed her moments of spite. I was disappointed not to have kissed my son goodnight. I rather rely on routine—tradition, as my mother might have said. After Evelyn left, I went into his room. The drawbridge had not been raised, and I wondered if he'd been waiting for me. He was perspiring in his pajamas, his damp hair dark against his temples, and I opened the window a few inches. I used to watch him sleep when he was a baby. It was the only time that I wasn't afraid.

When it started to come out in the trial, against my wishes, just so you know, Jimmy said Satan works in strange and mysterious ways, although never in a million years would he have suspected Mr. John Scanlon (my stepfather) was into that kind of thing. Then Jimmy went to my mom's house with a clipping shears, the kind you use in the yard, but the police had a officer there cause of all the sightseers, and he talked Jimmy into giving him the clippers. He didn't get in trouble cause the cop said he'd of done exactly the same thing. Later, Jimmy wanted me to talk about what happened, but I couldn't. He wanted details and stuff. I think it turned him on, but I just told him I couldn't remember any of it. And sometimes I couldn't.

Yesterday, Rafael, who is, as I said before, a really good dresser, told me my parts don't always match. We were on our way to a party on the beach at Malibu. When I said I did it on purpose, matching stripes with plaids, he said, I'm not talking about your clothes.

He's the kind of person you might think was gay if you didn't know him, which sort of makes sense when you know I really get along with gay guys. Deidra thought he was gay when she first met him, but she thinks everyone is gay. It's because of how he dresses, and his neatness, but also the things he's interested in, like antique helmets. I've never seen him in a pair of sweats, or even jeans, now that I think of it.

I explained to him I wear workout clothes all the time because I'm working out all the time. It's simple. If I don't have an audition or if I'm not working on a film, I'm working out. At least during the day. My trainer comes in the morning and takes me through my routine, including free weights. It lasts about two hours and then we go for a speed walk through the canyon, which is less fun cause he talks the whole time about the parts he's up for. He's first an actor and only second a personal trainer. He also sells drugs. When we're finished, I sometimes go for a facial, or a manicure with Chio in Beverly Hills, but the facial only if I don't have a lunch date in case there are marks on my face and I run into someone. Yoga is at five in the afternoon.

I usually stop by Deidra's after yoga. I can tell who's there based on the cars in her driveway. Usually it's her ex-husband or her manager. Her ex is an actor. We sit by the pool and watch the lights come on over L.A. and drink kir royales and talk about what's happening. He's never had a really big part, but he's never had one in life, either. He's in that group that follows Jack Nicholson around—old guys from New Jersey where Jack grew up, and basketball players, and guys he plays golf with, and guys who get the girls, and guys who get rid of the girls. Guys who overlap. How he got in with them is Deidra did a movie with Jack. Rafael calls it the rock-and-roll life—it takes five phone calls to find a restaurant you want to eat in that night, seven calls to change the restaurant, eight phone calls to change the time, eleven people who never show up, and six people you never saw before using your drugs. It makes Rafael anxious, but he's not from L.A.

Wanda's wife Jo is cooking tonight, and she asked if I wanted a plate brought to me. It's Mexican Night—tortillas and chips and beans. I didn't want to sound rude, so I just said I had a stomachache.

Jo is here for attacking her husband and hurting him permanently (the use of his legs) with a electric knife. She tried to cut them off. She found out he was dating a dolphin trainer he met when he took Jo and their two boys to SeaWorld in Florida. He told Jo the girl was the only trainer who didn't have sexual relations with the dolphins. Wanda thinks that part is funny, but I don't agree. Jo's husband divorced her when he heard she was with Wanda. She qualifies for a family furlough because she's been here at least two years, but he still won't see her. He minds more that she's with Wanda than her trying to cut his legs off.

She used to be a short-order cook in Bridgeport, Connecticut. Her whole life revolves around boiled water. She says she's only at peace when she's cooking eight hundred meals a day. Her goal when she gets out is to make a Dollar Breakfast. Her arms are short and muscular, maybe from so much frying. The wall behind her bed is covered with pictures of roast turkeys and hot-fudge sundaes and prime roasts with little white chefs' hats on the bones, plus a blonde woman in a tuxedo. What recipes she doesn't know by heart, she gets from *Prison Days* and *Gourmet* magazine.

When I bumped into Officer Cready today, bouncing along the gallery, he looked at me as if we shared a special understanding. When he said with a conspiratorial grin that Number 18 had tried to escape again, I realized that he assumes I share his feelings of contempt.

I questioned myself—am I so needful of acceptance that I invite this intimacy? I am able, so far, to acquit myself, even if I did have a drink with him. He simply cannot conceive that anyone working in the prison could be interested in the work—it's just a job, a frequently unpleasant job, that someone has to do, with good benefits negotiated by the union (does he think there is a Brotherhood of Psychiatrists?). I can't be too upset with him. As he would say, it's nothing personal. Dr. de la Vega told me that Cready's only steady employment before becoming a corrections officer was his yearly engagement as a Macy's Santa Claus.

My mother never liked Jimmy. She blames him for everything that happened, but she's wrong. I told her a hundred times we weren't always going to live that way. I remember how upset she was—my mom, of all people, who gave babies away—when she found the new baby tucked in the dishwasher space. We couldn't afford to put in the real dishwasher, and we thought it might as well be used for a good purpose. She could never forgive Jimmy for bragging to his dad he never once changed a Pampers. Maybe it reminded her of my real father. She was pregnant the third time when he left. I don't know if he ever even held me, let alone changed my diaper.

Jimmy never really knew what to do with me. He didn't know what to do with any of us, actually. He didn't even know what to do with HIMSELF, except work. And preach. We used to go to miniature golf in the beginning, but that didn't last long. There wasn't any time once the babies started coming. I didn't mind not doing things—there wasn't any money for extras, anyway. I just wanted to GET AWAY from Uncle Dad. That was all I cared about.

It's true I didn't want to get pregnant again after Shane. Even the doctor said it wasn't a good idea. I used to worry the electric shock they gave me could travel into a baby's brain, even if I wasn't pregnant yet. I could feel it all stored up in me, sizzling and ready, just waiting to jump out. Now Jimmy says the doctors should of diagnosed me better. He doesn't realize it would not of made any difference at all.

It didn't turn out very good, I know, but I tried my best. We both did. I can't put the blame on him. They wanted me to at the trial, but I couldn't. Until Jimmy and not counting Uncle Dad, no one else wanted me—and I'm not even sure Jimmy did. I don't think my mom cared much either way.

My patient Kai, a sullen Korean woman arrested with fifty-seven balloons of heroin in her lower intestine, rarely speaks, perhaps because her mouth is always stuffed with red fireball candies. She claims that the candy soothes the ulcers she contracted during her employment as a drug mule, and she is suing her employers in Hong Kong. Her mother, Soon, is also here—they were caught together at LaGuardia Airport. They look like sisters. They don't get along. They are the objects of much envy, as dozens of unsmiling relatives visit them every other week. Kai is much valued as a housekeeping porter. She earns fourteen cents an hour cleaning the chapel and the gym. There is a rumor that Kai has a friendship with one of the guards (she was in ad seg last month for a purported romance with the gentle Bangladeshi computer instructor formerly employed in the prison school).

The sexual tension that exists between all of the guards and all of the prisoners makes for constant speculation. The gossip dispels the potential for violence, as well as stimulates it, but it puts those women who are thought to be sexual conspirators with the guards, like Kai, on the side of the enemy. Even though the practicality of such an arrangement is recognized, it is still considered a betrayal. The women are known as bubble-gum whores—the officers give them the forbidden gum as a reward for sex. If an inmate is blowing bubbles, it is a sign that she has a relationship with one of the officers.

Dr. Forrest has a gorgeous flower on her desk. She says it is a lady's slipper orchid. Such a lovely name. She said it's been there for a month, but I never noticed it before. For the first time, I wish I had a window. I can smell the river these days, especially when the wind is blowing a certain way. At least I think I can smell it. Dr. Forrest would say my medicine has something to do with it, but I would say it's her. I measured the furniture again tonight and put the numbers in a new measurement book she gave me. A good day all around.

I ran into Captain Bradshaw again. I was on my way to the train station. It was raining. He was walking to his car. When I asked him how things were going, he said in his low, mocking voice, Just fine, doctor.

That's nice to know, I said. He makes me sweat and he knows it. Do you want to get a drink? I asked, surprising even myself. He looked at me and sighed. Sure, he said.

I went to the bar as he hung up our coats and said to the bartender in what I thought was a quiet voice, Would you give me a rather large vodka and tonic? when Captain Bradshaw appeared behind me. Yes, he said, and a rather large bourbon Manhattan. It's been a difficult day, I said, turning to face him. But then they're all difficult. I'm not doing too well.

You let them walk all over you, he said, running his hands through his wet hair. You make bargains I'd never consider making. Of course, women don't have much to offer. He lit a cigarette despite the NO SMOKING sign.

Not always, I said, a little startled. We don't always have less to offer. It sounded like an apology. I suddenly wondered if he might be a fanatic. The idea did not make him less appealing.

No, he said irritably. Of course, not always. Women are just not that valuable to prosecutors. No money? No information? No homey to trade? You'll be given a hard mandatory sentence. That's just a fact, doc. He stopped to take a drink. Women are more likely to use drugs than men, he said, and more serious drugs more often, whether it's selling or possession or committing crimes to support a habit. More drugs, but nothing to trade. That girl in 46 was an honor student at Marymount before she started using. She took one hit and the next thing she knew she was on the street hustling tricks.

He looked at his watch. He was in a bad mood, and his thoughts were elsewhere. Perhaps with the pretty college girl in 46. You going to Manhattan? he asked abruptly. Yes, I said,

I'm going to Manhattan. Come on, he said, finishing his drink, I'll walk you to the station. As we were leaving, I saw Dr. Henska, sitting in the back with a Latino guard I recognized from Building B. I pretended not to see them. She pretended not to see us, too.

The rain had stopped. We stood at the abandoned Victorian station house, despite my assurance that I didn't mind waiting alone. I found that I was staring at him, wondering if he might be the devil. Wondering if he might unfold a pair of wings and take off. In my nervousness, I began to quote the statistics for female filicide in Chicago.

Look, he said, interrupting me, they just weren't that crazy about sending you girls to the gas chamber. That's all.

So there's some advantage then, I said. In being female.

He looked at his watch again, but he smiled. Yes, he said, but it's changing. They're really starting to like it.

I was relieved when the train came. I looked for him from the window, but he was gone.

Sometimes I'm afraid, like when that new girl got slashed right next to me in the shower. If a woman is bigger than me, and looks at me funny, I always let her go first. I let her do whatever she wants, actually. Yesterday a woman told Keesha she liked her gold earrings. When Keesha said, Thanks, hon, the woman said, That means you're supposed to give them to me, bitch. Keesha knows how to be tough, but she just looked at the woman and said, You want my earrings? Fine. I just want to go home. She took the earrings out and threw them at her, and the woman had to scramble for them on her hands and knees on the wet floor, her big butt in the air. It was pretty funny, but Keesha wasn't smiling, so I wasn't, either.

I have a new patient named Priscilla. She is seven months pregnant, and her presence in the prenatal unit has upset the women greatly. Despite their absolutely unshakable (and inaccurate) belief that a child will instinctively recognize its natural mother, the fear of loss and usurpation is so strong that many of them, like Keesha, abandon a child rather than suffer the pain of losing it. When Aida is not in solitary, she calls her children every day, dutifully making each telephone reservation twenty-four hours in advance. If she misses one day, as is often unavoidable, her six children punish her by refusing to visit her. Some women have never called home, convinced that they will hear bad news. Larissa in Number 50 is known never to have used the telephone after she received the news that her daughter burned to death one Sunday morning.

My mom had a hard life. She quit school in the ninth grade and went to work for a Polish family restaurant on Long Island where she stayed for thirty years. My grandma worked her whole life in a pants factory in New Jersey. I myself couldn't wait to go to work, mainly cause it meant I'd get out of the house. I left school when Jimmy wouldn't let me get a abortion, and I went to work at Wal-Mart. Actually, I had a interview there for a summer job and that's how I knew I was pregnant in the first place, from the drug tests they make you take. They must not of minded I was pregnant cause they hired me anyway. I was surprised—I never in a million years thought I'd pass all those tests. The questions are pretty tricky, like, When did you last steal something? Even if you did not steal something, you have to think fast to answer that one, and unless you're real stupid, who's going to say, Oh, yeah, last week at Victoria's Secret. One of the other questions was, Some people can work better when they're a little high, yes or no? Another was, Do you need to go against the system to get ahead? I said, I don't know to the first, and no to the second. I wasn't trying to be cute, that's just what I thought they wanted me to say. I must of done okay cause there I was five days later folding sweaters in the ladies' department.

Being at work each day wasn't that different from being at school. Up in the morning, breakfast, dropped at the mall by my brother, work, lunch, work, take the bus home. Jimmy and I weren't married yet. It was pretty tiring even though I didn't do that much. I just picked things up and folded them or hung them on hangers. I was surprised how messy people are. We are messy at home, but I didn't know people were messy in public.

You're not allowed to leave your section at Wal-Mart, and if you do for some reason, like to get something in another department, you get in trouble. I made friends with a very nice person named Mrs. Mercer, who was a widow at a young age with five kids when her husband died suddenly. She was a friend to me through thick and thin. While we folded, she'd tell me the stories of the daytime soap operas up until the present time, and then, because we were missing the new episodes, she'd make them up. She was good at it, and it made the day go fast. I wish she was here now.

She used to say, Are you sure about this guy? Meaning Jimmy. He was the only boyfriend or husband who came by while we were working. Sometimes he'd just stand there, hidden in the dresses. It would make me jump when I looked around and finally noticed him. Mrs. Mercer would say, What is WITH him? And I would just shrug and laugh. He wanted to check up on me. I don't know what he thought he'd find. He dropped in while he was doing his church missionary work so it's not like it was out of his way, but still. I didn't mind it like she did. I liked the attention.

I never had a boyfriend before Jimmy. He didn't know about Uncle Dad, but Uncle Dad sure knew about him. He was jealous of him. Once Uncle Dad said he'd tell everyone what me and him were doing and ruin my life, and I had to promise I'd always be his little girl to calm him down. Like when I was small and he'd volunteer to give me a bath when my mother came home tired. Sometimes she was so beat she'd start cooking dinner without taking her coat off, just go straight to the stove and start boiling water. I used to think, Some fine day, it won't be like this.

Over the years, Ellie and me figured out ways to trick Uncle Dad, like sending Ellie in my place. He didn't like her as much as he liked me, and that was a problem. He'd act mean when I sent Ellie instead. I got pretty good at telling lies, which was helpful when it came to things like taking the test at Wal-Mart. I just tried to say what Ellie would say under the circumstances and, as I mentioned, I must of done okay, because there I was, folding.

I called Jimmy twice this month, but he wouldn't accept the charges.

I looked for Captain Bradshaw this morning, but I didn't see him. It was snowing. The large snowflakes drifted slowly into the prison courtyard, then rose again on a draft of air from the laundry. As Helen would say, it was lovely.

I was standing in my cell in the dark tonight when two of the officers started talking. It was the same voices as the other time. I guess they don't care if you hear them. What could you do about it anyway.

One of the voices said, You remember I said she was stuck-up? You got to trust me on this—she thinks she's hot shit. The other voice, the one I recognize, the nice one, said, What'd you do, you fat fuck. You asked her out again? He started to laugh. And the other voice said, What the fuck are you talking about? The voice I think of as the greasy one. And the nice voice said, She's way out of your league, pal, and the fat voice said, Yours, too, asshole. Just in case you were thinking about it. And the nice voice laughed even harder.

I had an audition at HBO in Burbank for a new series about cowgirls. I lied and said I could ride horses, but everyone lies about that. When I left HBO, I drove to Santa Monica to the speech therapist. One of the things they make you do for a speech problem is call people on the phone and ask about prices and things, like a limousine company. How much to the airport? How much to Burbank? How much to bring your dog? You're supposed to say right off, Hello, I lisp, or Hello, I stutter, or Hello, I whatever, but that I could never do. I have way too much pride. People are nicer to you supposedly when you admit your defects. There was a guy at my gym, before I got a personal trainer, which is what I should've done in the first place, who used to make fun of me, imitating me when I would mess up a word, like wunning machine. He wanted to fuck me, I know, but he was also Romanian, and that's what Romanians do, make fun of the retarded and anyone with any kind of disability, not that a speech impediment is in that category. Anyway, I don't really have a problem anymore, and that's the good news. The bad news is I didn't get the part.

I was just finishing a disappointing book by the poet H.D. about her analysis with Freud when the doorman rang to say that I had a visitor. It was ten o'clock on a Friday night, and I was already in my pajamas. I raced to the closet to put on jeans and a shirt and consequently opened the door to Captain Bradshaw a little out of breath. He followed me into the living room, and as I turned to ask if he'd like something to drink, I saw him take in everything—the book, the margarita glass, my worn slippers, the catalogs from J. Crew and Pottery Barn, and the rather large photograph of Ransom on the desk. That's my son, I said. I hope so, he said.

It's been a while since I had a man in my apartment. I've spent so much time alone that I've lost altogether the small confidence I've been hoarding since girlhood. More than that. To be honest, I've forgotten how to make love. This has happened before, particularly when attempting to do something I haven't done in some time—I forget how to pack for a trip, how to give a dinner party, how to write a letter of condolence. When I realized last year that I no longer remembered how to have sexual intercourse, however, I asked my friend Miranda for advice. Her instructions were disappointing.

I, convinced that I'd forgotten how to experience pleasure, if I'd ever known (I couldn't really judge by Rafael), was advised to keep a small compact with mirror, a lipstick, and a dispenser of Tic Tacs on the floor by my side of the bed, items to which I'd have recourse upon awaking half an hour—this was an important detail—before my companion. I'm embarrassed to say that I did exactly as I was told, hiding the specified items under the bed, although I substituted lip gloss for lipstick. Unfortunately, my hangover was so severe I not only did not wake before the gentleman (my new lawyer) who'd spent the night, but did not hear him leave. So my assurance was not running high when Bradshaw made a quick survey of my living room.

I didn't have any bourbon or gin to give him, and I offered him a margarita. He lit a cigarette. I leapt to my feet to find something that could pass as an ashtray and found a delicate clay bowl that Ransom had taken five months to make in first grade. I watched, impressed by the alacrity of my betrayal, as Bradshaw put his ashes in my son's present to me.

I'm sorry about the other night, he said. The night it was raining. I just found out my wife was moving to Miami with my kid. She says she can't handle the foreigners at the airport anymore.

I hope she likes Cubans, I said.

She's convinced they all have anthrax and they're bringing it here on purpose to kill us. Suicide sick people. He sighed. She says the beauty pageants for kids are better in Florida, anyway.

He looked stricken, his eyes a little wild. I poured us both another drink. I was too embarrassed to speak. I was elated that he was there, but I was sure I was perspiring visibly, which worried me. There certainly was a lot of moisture on my palms. As I jumped up to shut the door to the hall, suddenly fearful that we'd wake Ransom, he said, Just so you know, doc, corrections officers are the dentists of law.

He'd just come from Sloatsburg. He, too, must be of the view that a day in prison leaves one suffused with a noxious odor because he asked if he could take a shower. I gave him a clean towel and a new bar of soap (quickly unwrapped, teeth gnawing the plastic wrapping, leaving a bad taste in my mouth) and left him in the bathroom while I finished what remained of the margaritas.

When I stepped into the shower, he did not seem surprised, although I don't believe his intention had been to wash us both. I was very nervous. I'd never done anything like it before. He had. He has a round red scar on his left shoulder. His penis is small. Not so small as to be a detriment, but small all the same. I stood on my toes, my back to him. He didn't say a word. His hands were on my hips. My eyes were closed, and the sound of the water, and the feel of it on my face and breasts, rendered him anonymous. He knows how to do it. I wondered if he'd ever had sexual intercourse with a prisoner. I find that I have rather vivid fantasies about that. I imagined him making love to LizAnn in her cell. Then I imagined him making love to me in a cell. He *was* making love to me.

Afterward, he dried me. Between my legs, under my arms. I wanted to look into his eyes, but the thoroughness of his examination did not allow for it. We made love again on the sofa. I think that I said thank you when he left.

The next day, Ransom and I were watching a National Geographic special on manatees when he drew a pair of my underpants from behind a sofa cushion with the tips of two fingers. What's this? he asked. Oh, thank you, darling, I said, I've been looking for those. He dropped them onto the coffee table and I slipped them into my pocket.

I thought about him all weekend.

Dr. Forrest warned me my new medicine could make me stop dreaming. I remember when I was breastfeeding Kaley and she was getting me up every three hours. The baby doctor said I wasn't dreaming and people who don't dream can go insane. I was so happy with my baby, so in love with her, I didn't mind being up all night, even when I was worn out from the events of the day. I wanted to be with her EVERY SECOND. It made me not afraid of the night. Sitting in the darkness feeding her, I was never afraid. The doctor said I was exhausting her, letting her nurse too long, but what would he know. I was the mother and I would never hurt her. I would have died for that baby. I loved her so much I couldn't of slept if I wanted to.

Cready's Tip for March: Lifers make better inmates than short timers. Short timers don't care about punishment cause they've been in trouble their whole sorry life. Lifers have usually done one bad thing once. And they're not going anywhere.

I don't see my husband Jimmy very much anymore. He's so busy at the computer store and with his charity work there isn't much time to get away. It's a three-hour drive one way just to get here anyway. My mom says he was promoted last month so I guess the time he's putting in is worth it. He did have enough time, though, to send me a article about postpartum depression. It's called "The Helpmate Tells How He Was Affected," and this is what it says: "I admit the unfair burden of her and the children left me emotionally and physically drained. For four years I had to juggle my essential lay work and my even more important responsibilities as a congregation elder and on top of that be a husband and a father! Happily, I was able to adjust my secular work so I could be home earlier, especially on the nights we attended Christian meetings, as Noreen unfortunately needed me at home to help prepare dinner and dress the children and feed the new baby. Because of my juggling, we were still able, thank the Lord, to attend meetings. In time, I learned to be patient with my wife. I learned she wanted to be hugged. What she didn't want was logic (1 Thessalonians 5:14)."

I realize that for the first time in almost a year I'm not thinking about the women. Now I find myself distracted by the niceties that engage the attention of a middle-class lady who's getting laid—my Brazilian wax, for example. I didn't think about such things when I was married to Rafael. Until Ransom was born, all that I wanted was to study and to sleep. Even after Ransom was born. So this, I say to myself in amazed triumph, is what I needed! All those years with the troll-like Professor Cluff when what I really wanted was a pedicure. That chilly Palo Alto summer spent on a theory of moral rationalism when what I wanted was new underwear. New sheets.

I'm even different in bed. Less manipulative in my passivity, less impatient. I've stopped dreaming about my mother— I hope not forever; it's the only time that I see her. I've certainly stopped thinking of ways to torment Rafael. I owe him an apology. For the first time, I'm not so anxious about my son. I probably owe him an apology, too, but that can wait.

. . .

Dr. Forrest's been in a good mood lately. It's sure a relief from a month ago. She used to worry me when she'd ask how you go about cutting yourself. She once asked me if you could just use a normal razor!

Because of the community bathroom here, I have a spreading fungus on my feet, even though I always wear my plastic shoes in the shower. Dr. Subramaniya gave me a prescription for some cream, but the pharmacy is out of it and doesn't know when they'll get it. Maybe never, they said. My big toe measures one and three-eighths inches, my second toe is one and one-eighth inches, the next is also one and one-eighth inches, the fourth is one and one-sixteenth inches, and the baby toe is just one inch. On the left foot, the big toe is one and one-fourth inches, the second is one and one-eighth inches, the third is one and one-sixteenth inches, the fourth is one inch, and the little toe is seven-eighths of an inch.

Wanda told me Dr. Forrest's first name is Louise. Wanda knows everything. They let me have knitting needles today.

I'm not usually impulsive. It must be all the crap I'm going through with my wife. I notice it at work, too, letting things go that I'd usually be all over, like Jessie holding my hand. I like Jessie all right—she makes me laugh—I just don't want to hold her hand. She's not supposed to touch me anyway. Sloatsburg is known as an easy place to do time. It's one of the reasons I wanted to work here in the first place. I really don't need to be kicking the shit out of child molesters all day long. I've done that already.

She'd just changed from her pajamas—they were on the bathroom floor—which might explain the sweating. She kept wiping her hands. Maybe it was the moisture from the glass—she was drinking as fast as she could. When I asked her why she was whispering, she said her kid was asleep down the hall.

She has a nice body. Pretty body. Really white. She mustn't get out much. She had hair under her arms, but I think she'd have shaved if she'd known I was coming. Her pubic hair was soft and silky. I told her so, and she said, You must know Spanish girls, and I didn't say anything. I saw her looking at my cock when we were in the shower. It would have bothered me once, not being as endowed as I'd like. When I first got out of the police academy twenty years ago, I made my partner promise to cover my body if anything happened to me. I didn't want anyone laughing at me when I was dead. Especially when I was dead. I don't feel that way anymore. About the laughing.

There is a hum about her, coming out of her body, like a little electric station in the snow. I kept wondering what she was thinking. She has a strange way of looking at you, her eyes shining. I wouldn't want to be one of her patients. That combination of ladylike and spooked would get to you.

When she got into the shower, I can't say I was expecting her, but looking back I can see it's a good move—ask a girl if you can take a shower in her apartment and then see what happens. At least one of you is naked right away. I don't even know why I did it. I'd more or less decided not to sleep with anyone until this mess with Shelagh is straightened out—I had this idea I needed to be at my best, like an athlete. A divorced man in training. I wasn't even that dirty. I'd had a couple of cocktails earlier in the evening with my about-to-be-ex-brother-in-law, but not enough to require a shower.

She'd been reading before I got there, and she'd marked her place with a postcard of the Golden Gate Bridge. When I was leaving, I said I'd call her, but from the look in her eyes I could see she wasn't going to hold her breath. Good.

When I talk to Dr. Forrest about Shane and Kaley, the feelings of love that are always there rise up inside me so strong that it hurts to breathe. It's like the love and the sadness is unbearable. It used to mix me up that all that sadness could go so easily with love, but I am understanding it better now.

Dr. Forrest says she is trying to help me see that everything I did came from SOMEPLACE. I wasn't just evil or a bad mother. There are reasons for everything I did. She says the chemicals in my brain act on me in all kinds of ways. If I hallucinate it's because of what happens in my brain. I was with her up till then, but then I got confused again.

These THINGS are so real to me or, as she would put it, so NECESSARY TO ME, I can't have imagined them. If the Horsemen aren't real, then I am just insane. The Horsemen believed in me, and I believed in them. They have been with me since I was a little girl. The idea that I might of imagined them, well, I deserve to die if that is true. If the Messengers are made up, and it was me who made them up, then I won't even get to be with my babies. I will be drowning in the Burning Pits of Hell.

. . .

All my life, I've been trying too hard. I'm doing it now with Bradshaw. Always a little ahead of the game. It's why I was never a good tennis player. Or a good dancer. (I don't even want to think about sex.) Oh, I could hit the ball—my mother saw to that—but I was always in front of it, and not in a good way. It was a disappointment to her, I know. She was the most graceful person in the world.

When she died, I proceeded to drive my father crazy by staring at him. I was so afraid of displeasing him that I never took my eyes from him. Before I was sent away to school, I was expected to appear at lunch parties on the weekend, the only child at the table. When, in the middle of a story, my father would pause to see if I, too, was engaged in bright talk, I did not fail to gratify him by my animation. I'd taught myself to mouth a silent conversation, and the instant I saw him look my way, I'd go to work. After lunch, he would say, in front of the bewildered guests, You really did well today, Louise.

Because I'd learned to interpret his moods by watching him so closely, I concluded that I could read his thoughts. This fanciful assumption did not give me confidence and composure but, quite the contrary, caused me distress. I never assumed that this gift was mine alone but one that could be achieved by anyone willing to concentrate. It was only a matter of paying attention. I lived in fear that he might someday decide to do so himself, with the result that he'd be able to read my mind, too. I cannot imagine which of my thoughts I feared would alarm my fairly harmless father—perhaps all of them. It was not anger or resentment that shamed me and made me furtive, but my constant, wearying grief. My mother's death had crushed me.

It was a relief when he married and had another child, a daughter, allowing me to slip away without regret. It would be convenient to blame him for the isolation of my girlhood, but not very fair. I don't hold him responsible for much. It is thanks to him that I determined that the essential thing was to be alone— alone and useful—and despite my sense of general peril, my loneliness became essential to me. At least, I convinced myself that it was so, and eventually it became a habit.

We know about the part love plays in the origin of conscience. Whether or not you actually kill your father is not the decisive thing. Wishing it is really quite sufficient.

Cready's Special St. Patrick's Day Tip: Schizophrenics are one percent of the worldwide population. Check it out. The important thing is to be able to pick one out in a crowd.

I had another audition this morning so I stayed over at Deidra's. I don't want to do any more TV, but it's pilot season and my manager keeps setting up auditions even though he knows TV is the kiss of death for a movie career. I told him I only want to go up for movies or HBO, but he can't help himself, and I guess I can't either, cause I keep going. Deidra talks me into it, too, but she has a soft spot for sitcoms. She says her series made her, and she's right.

I rushed to the Valley to pick up the script and then rushed back to Deidra's. I spent the rest of the morning going over my lines. Deidra herself refuses to read lines, which is a pain. I was up for the part of a woman with three kids whose husband runs off with another woman. It's a comedy, actually. I took a slug of Tussionex and rushed back to Universal for the audition. It was boiling hot in the Valley. The Santa Ana wind is back, and I had sand up my nose and in my eyes.

I had a pass to get on the lot, and the guard gave me directions to the director's office, which was in a Spanish bungalow behind the tower. There was one other girl waiting in the office when I got there, which was much better than usual. There's usually thirty identical girls trying not to stare at each other, but this girl was the complete opposite of me in every way, including not that pretty, so I forgot about her and went over my lines for the thousandth time. I waited for an hour, and then the receptionist said, Oh, I'm supposed to take you to his trailer. You have ten minutes while they set up the next shot. Which is what they always say.

The trailer was parked next to the soundstage. I went up the steps and sat inside at one of those little built-in tables between the director and a lady casting director who was reading *Us* magazine. It was like sitting at a shelf. We were only inches apart. Give me a sec, the casting director said, putting down the magazine, I haven't seen these pages yet. We sat there while she read the scene. It was stifling even with the air-conditioning on. No one offered me anything, not even a glass of water. The director lit a cigarette. He was distracted, looking at his phone and sending text messages and laughing at what he sent. He wasn't interested in small talk. It was too hot to talk anyway.

I was probably the twentieth actor he'd seen that day. We sat there as she read the pages, and then he finally said, Okay, babe, can we go?

The scene was of the woman finding out her husband has left her. I go from happiness to complete hysteria in half a page. I was so close I spit all over her—luckily she was holding the pages in front of her face. She never once put them down, so at least she didn't get wet. The cigarette smoke was burning my eyes. I was already feeling a little woozy and I felt like I was going to throw up. I tried to remember everything Mrs. Scott taught us about making a fourth wall between you and the audience. That's what you're supposed to do when you're onstage—make an invisible barrier so it's not like a talk show. I'd just got to the middle of the scene when someone knocked on the door, making me jump a foot in the air, which wasn't easy considering how packed we were. The director put out his cigarette in his Coke can, and thanked me and left.

When I opened the door, there was the girl who'd been sitting in the office with me. How'd it go, she whispered as I came down the stairs. You were fantastic, the casting director yelled after me, holding the door open just a crack so the heat wouldn't get in. I could tell the girl was really nervous. I'm reading for the mom's part, she said. Don't worry, I said, you'll be great, and I kind of meant it.

I didn't feel like going straight home, not after that, so I went back to Deidra's. She wasn't there. I put my nightgown and sweater back on and got into bed in the freezing cold bedroom and waited for her to come home. Some days are better than others.

. . .

I drove into the city tonight after work, calling her from my car. She said to come over. Her son was spending the night with a friend who lives in their building.

We sat in her living room. She'd made martinis in a glass pitcher with its own glass stick for stirring. As I sat there, I wondered if we were on the verge of something. I could tell she was thinking it, too. She stared at my hands whenever I reached for my glass or lit a cigarette, and I thought, If you knew what these hands have done, and where these hands have been, you'd be less happy about them. And then I thought, She's a shrink. She *does* know. It made me feel good to sit with her, which is funny cause I wouldn't have thought that's what I wanted. I didn't feel like talking. I thought about fucking her, but there wasn't enough time. I had to be back in Yonkers by eight.

I'm a little worried about you, I said as I got up. I don't know where it came from. The martinis, LizAnn's parole, my cunt of a wife—everything was spinning around in my head and I was having a hard time holding it together.

Worried? she said, drawing herself up in that way people do when they think you're criticizing them.

Not in a bad way, I said. I just have a feeling you're going to get in trouble.

She smiled, and I could see she was relieved. You mean with you, she said. That's funny. Because I was just going to ask if you wanted to go to bed.

No, I said. Not in trouble with me.

Oh, she said, looking away, and her face got red.

I kissed her goodbye and left.

. . .

It's St. Patrick's Day. In the kitchen they will dye everything they can get their hands on green—green cottage cheese, green fruit cocktail, green rice. I won't be eating any of it, even if it wasn't green.

I was supposed to give Wanda my answer about being in her family, and I did. This is a big step for me. I never knew a lesbian in my life, and if I did, I didn't know it. I said I'd be honored to be in her family. There is a ceremony in the beginning of next month to introduce me. Wanda always gives you something religious when you join—I got a blue medal of Saint Christopher carrying a baby.

It's the Catholics who wear medals usually, but that doesn't bother me. Uncle Dad's first wife was a Catholic so his children with her were brought up Catholic. I was always a little jealous of their school uniform—Patty's was a green plaid jumper and a little white blouse with a collar. I don't know if Uncle Dad ever made his own girls do the things he made me and Ellie do, but my guess is he didn't. They didn't live with us, but I think I'd of known if he did. Ellie definitely knows, but she's not telling. She's good at keeping secrets.

I guess I am beginning to know certain things myself now, even if I fight against it. I don't say REMEMBER because Dr. Forrest says I never FORGOT. She says for most of my life I wouldn't let myself know. She is only partly right. She thinks she knows everything, but there are things I haven't told her. It would begin in the tub. He would turn out the light in the bathroom while he was giving me a bath and it was the strangest feeling being in that warm water in the darkness.

It was like it was all around you, but you couldn't tell what it was—were you floating in darkness or were you floating in water? It was different when he came to my room. Then I was floating in air, looking down at us. Later, after I had Shane and Kaley, he would come by when Jimmy was at work. I was floating then, too, but that was because of the medicine Dr. Kyrgorin gave me. He stopped for a while after Shane was born, but not for long. I thought it was because I lost my figure, and I got back in shape as fast as I could—that is a example of what Dr. Forrest says happens to people. The person who is abused wants her abuser to like her. When I thought about that, I knew it was true, but when Dr. Forrest first said it, I couldn't admit it. It just made me so sad. I cried for days after that. Some things are very terrible.

Ransom and I went to see the armor at the Met today. After September 11, we were going once a week, but we haven't been in a while. He is partial to the samurai helmets of the sixteenth century, and I don't blame him. The body armor with its vulnerability at the knee and elbow joints upsets him—he cannot understand why the armorers did not better protect the warriors in their keeping, despite the need for mobility, although the elegant cones made for the ears of the warhorses make him very happy.

In the past, my son's passion for the historical implements of defense, rather than for dinosaurs or anime figures or skateboards, caused me some concern. His interest has afforded me much arcane information about armor, rather than, say, the habits of stegosaurus or Princess Aoki, and I like that aspect of it. Thanks to Ransom, I know it is a misconception that the smallness of armor reflects the size of Renaissance horsemen—much of the smaller armor was used by children training in the art of war.

Ransom has been influenced by his father. That Rafael is obsessed with the fortification of medieval keeps and the forging of damascene rapiers is not in itself a compelling puzzle, but his refusal to enlighten me over the years has been a disappointment. The very fact of my profession inhibits him. Something scared the daylights out of Rafael when he was a boy—that much seems clear—yet the very facility of such an assumption makes me wince. I work hard not to draw easy conclusions, which made it particularly frustrating that Rafael would never tell me his story. He was, however, as I often remind myself, my husband, not my patient. His mother is dead. That's all that I know.

As we walked through the gallery, Ransom asked me what emblem I would choose for a helmet were I the leader of a samurai clan. I said that I liked the gold sickle moon very much. He himself, at least this afternoon, chose the stylized rabbit ears, two feet long. It's funny, he said, but rabbits aren't supposed to be brave.

Like other creatures, I said. Children, for example.

He looked at me.

You're brave, I said.

Yes, he said after a moment. But I live in a fort.

We'd stopped before a model of a charger, heavily caparisoned in steel mesh and faded red damask, once used in battle by Gustavus III of Sweden. If they're here, Ransom said with a sigh of relief, it means they're okay.

I didn't understand.

If they made it this far, he said, a hint of impatience in his voice, they're okay. Like this horse.

Yes, I said. I see what you mean. I took his hand.

Nothing can hurt this horse now, he said.

No, I said. And nothing is going to hurt you. I hope you know that.

He said nothing, and we moved to the next exhibit, a handsome suit of embossed armor, typical, I've come to learn, of the school of Milan. He did not pull his hand from mine as he sometimes does, and I was grateful for it.

When I came on guard duty yesterday, there was a note on the bulletin board that one of the women in 47 has been diagnosed with AIDS. That would be Keesha. She was thrown into an observation cell following the results of her tests. She then tore the cell apart, injuring herself. She wasn't sent to ad seg thanks to Subramaniya, who asked that she not be punished, considering the circumstances. The warden must have been in a good mood.

There are other women here with HIV, and there are weekly support meetings. In some prisons, they charge those inmates with incurable diseases for their meds so they won't ask for special treatment. When prisoners were first diagnosed with HIV, their food, when prepared by their fellow inmates, was soaked in piss and mixed with ground glass. No one would speak to them or touch them. The National Guard was sent to prisons to protect them from the other prisoners. Or was it vice versa? Molina says he can't remember. I wasn't here yet, thank God.

When Keesha refused to leave her cell, the warden—not in such a good mood anymore—ordered five officers in riot gear to remove her. The boys were in their special forced-cell-extraction suits—they looked like they were going to Mars. They're scared to death of infection. They left a big mess in her cell, cutting open her pillow and mattress and emptying her locker onto the floor. We used to do that when we were cops, but at least you'd find something to steal.

Molina seemed even more fucked-up than usual. When I asked him what was going on, he said, Fucking A, man. Methadone and bad coke.

My patient Mary is an elderly black woman in prison for killing her middle-aged son in a struggle over a kitchen knife with which he was torturing her. She will be imprisoned for the rest of her life, a victim of conflicting interests in which the instinct of self-preservation was uncustomarily stronger than the maternal. Some of the younger women scorn her old-fashioned ways—she listens to tapes of the Mississippi Mass Choir on her headphones and hands out stained recipes for sweet potato pie. The headphones also serve to conceal the ruffled scar tissue of the ear removed by her son.

No matter what I say, Mary nods gravely as though con-firmed in an opinion she has long held. Her ability to get on with the staff is mocked by the others. They call her Clarisse Thomas, after the Supreme Court justice. She suffers from mi-graines, which occasionally interrupt a game of checkers she's been playing for seven years with successive roommates. She pays her commissary bill with her winnings. When she has one of her headaches, she drapes a blanket over her head. It is Mary who said to me, Once they cut you, they cut you forever.

There's one of those Tom Hanks movies on tonight, which is what they always show. It's so we won't get overexcited. They put it on in the chapel. I've never gone before, but now I'm allowed out of my cell, I might consider it. You have to get there two hours early to find a seat, and then all of them are saved anyway. If you go after unlock, you might find a place on the side. Wanda says there wasn't a seat left last time. The best seats are in front cause the guards can't see what you're doing, although they KNOW what is going on, not just the kissing. It's just understood, so long as you don't make any trouble.

It doesn't matter to me where I sit because no way I'm doing anything anyway. I just don't want to look like I think I'm spe-cial. They said that girl was raped last month because she needed to be taught a LESSON. Wanda won't be there so maybe I won't go. She can't have movie privileges for ten days cause they say she had a cross-conversation with someone else's visitor. There were fourteen people in the Visit Room, three people at four desks, plus two officers, and she says she didn't speak to a single person except for her mom and her six-year-old daughter. Last month, Number 39 lost her visiting privileges for two weeks because she was staring at a male visitor's crotch.

A big piece of evidence at Wanda's trial was a tape of her talking to her dead husband at the cemetery. Which she and a lot of others thinks is illegal even if the FBI was involved (her husband was a big shot in a Puerto Rican gang). I agree. A conversation with a dead person should definitely be off-limits. A girl named Bethany got into trouble last month ordering drugs on the telephone. She didn't know the sign saying RECORDED means they are listening. It's so loud I don't know how anyone can hear anything anyway.

Keesha didn't get any letters from her pen pals this month. She thinks someone must of told them about the HIV.

He watched in silence as I finished my second martini in half an hour. I'd been thinking incessantly about sleeping with him, if that is what you can call it. I hate to admit it, but the prison has stimulated me sexually.

If you don't mind, I said, I'd really prefer not to talk about the women tonight. I need a rest from them. They've taken over my life. (As have you, I thought, but I didn't say that.)

He was drinking bourbon, and he stood to make himself another drink. You're getting in too deep, he said.

I looked at him—he doesn't customarily give words a stronger meaning than they can bear. I wondered if he was angry with me. The idea of his anger excited me. Sometimes, I said, jumping up, I put myself in LizAnn's place, or Shirley's, or even Helen's place, and I think, Could I have done that? How would I have killed that man? Would I have done it with a knife? A gun? I dream about them every night. In the dreams, I'm locked in a cell for the rest of my life. What is more terrible than the loss of freedom is the feeling that I deserve it.

Look, he said, you're a little confused. It's what happens. I've seen it before.

I felt a flash of resentment that he could compare me with anyone else. I wanted him to think that there was no one like me. In the beginning, I said, rushing on, Helen was difficult for me. There were times when I thought of asking Dr. Fischl to take her as a patient. I thought she was too crazy, even for me. I used to be afraid of Darla, too, but we have a friendship now. She tells me how to be a sex slave, and I tell her how to differentiate object relations. She attributes her success with men to not having a gag reflex.

I thought you didn't want to talk about them, he said.

Before I could answer, not that I had an answer I wanted to give him, his cell phone rang. It was his wife. If he didn't pack up what remained of his belongings, she was going to throw them into the street.

This isn't what I intended, I said when he put away his phone. Just so you know. It's not what I was trained to do.

I know, he said. That's what worries me.

I managed to keep him for another half hour.

. . .

I'm really excited! I got a part in a movie about the Mexican Revolution. I already started my diet. I'm supposed to be really thin—the girl is kept prisoner by a General Zapata (great name) for six months. Rafael is doing the sets. My fingers are crossed we get to go to Cancún or someplace. Ransom could visit us. I've never been out of the States before. It would be good for Ransom to see how this business works. When he was here last Christmas, I wanted to take him to a birthday party in Santa Barbara my agent was giving for his twelve-year-old godson who is a model. Ransom himself could easily be a model, but my big plans came to naught when Rafael said absolutely not, no way, forget about it.

We went instead to a party at Deidra's to celebrate her ex-husband's marriage—a celebration cause Deidra wouldn't be paying alimony anymore. There were ten people in the living room, sitting around the glass coffee table. We put Ransom in Deidra's media room with a bunch of DVDs and locked him in. Deidra's massage guy—he's so big he has trouble judging distances—bumped her arm when she was making some lines, and the coke spilled into a crystal candy dish. I thought Pepe was going to lick every single gumball until she screamed at him to get away. Deidra made more lines, one for everyone else, and two for herself. She was in a bad mood cause she'd been trying to get her driver Mohammed to change his name, and when he wouldn't do it, she had to fire him.

While we were sitting there, Rafael picked up a book about Steve Wynn's museum in Las Vegas and went out by the pool to read, which I told him later was not a good career move. If he wants to keep working in this town, he can't act like he thinks he's better than everyone else, even if he is. It wasn't the book, I explained, or even not doing drugs, but going outside and sitting alone by the pool. Deidra gave me a look when he went, which I pretended not to see. Deidra may be my best friend, but I'm still loyal. What I said to Rafael when we got home is another thing.

It turns out Rafael was right about not taking Ransom to the model's party. Too many gay agents now that Mike Ovitz has left CAA, not that they bother me. Ransom's just at that age when it could go either way, so why tempt him.

Keesha's really sick. It just happened so quick. Like me when I found out I was pregnant. My mom said she never saw anyone in her whole life look pregnant faster than me. It's true I blew up fast. One reason was it kept certain people away from me (not Jimmy) and the other reason is I ate and ate. It was like I was trying to blow us both up. I wanted us to explode together.

Keesha says as many years as she's spent in prison, she never thought she'd die here. She figures she got sick from her last pimp who liked to hot-rail crystal meth and then take a couple Viagra. The meth made his teeth crumble up. She knew he was having sex, her included, about ten times a day—what she didn't know is he was poz. I stopped doing my Christmas gifts so I could knit a hat for her—it's red, green, and yellow, the color of the Rasta flag, like she likes. Dr. Subramaniya has her on a lot of medicine and isn't charging her extra for it. He's a very nice man.

Dr. Forrest has been spending a lot of time with her, too. Some people say they should let you out of here if you have AIDS.

Speaking of doctors, my mom wrote and told me Jimmy is suing Dr. Kyrgorin.

Dr. de la Vega came to my office today to ask to be removed from the case of an inmate in Building A named Kim. She is in her fourth year of a ten-year sentence for second-degree murder. Kim assisted her mother in the killing of her school friend Judy, who was staying with them while her parents spent the summer on the Gulf Coast of Texas, where they operated a booth in a traveling circus. Judy's siblings, a set of fraternal twins and a little girl disabled by infantile polio, were already in foster care.

Kim's attorney has filed an appeal for a new trial, as Kim is demonstrably unsound of mind. She is Dr. de la Vega's patient and it is his testimony that will be used in court. Dr. de la Vega, however, is having second thoughts. He admitted to me, his head in his hands, that he cannot bear the sight of her and feels himself incapable of rendering an impartial judgment. I told him that he was under no obligation, morally or professionally (Is there any difference? he asked, moaning), to continue his treatment of the patient. As much as I can't stand the sight of her, he said, his hands shaking, I hate the victim more.

An emaciated Judy was found dead in a bathtub with the words I'M A SICK WHORE AND PROUD OF IT! cut into her chest. The "s" of sick was carved backward. Kim's mother was assisted in torturing the girl by three other children, ten, eleven, and twelve years old, as well as her daughter, Kim. When one of the boys had trouble spelling the word whore, Kim wrote it in big block letters for him on a piece of homework later used as evidence. Kim's mother complained of Judy's lack of cleanliness. The girl was tied to her bed at night to punish her for soiling the bed. When she dirtied the bed, as was inevitable, she was forced to eat her own excrement. When she vomited, she was made to eat her vomit. Kim testified that they made her dance naked for them, a Dr Pepper bottle dangling from her vagina. She was beaten so badly one night that she lost consciousness, which is when they put her into the bath.

What disturbs Dr. de la Vega is that the dead girl did nothing to save herself. He cannot bear it, and his distress causes him to entertain his own fantasies of torture, which alarm him. He is so angry with her for not going to the police, for not running away, for not fighting back, that he cannot sleep at night. I understood how deeply he was affected when he said, gazing at me as if he had never seen me before, She could have called me. Why didn't she just pick up the phone and call me?

I sent Dr. de la Vega home for the rest of the week. He can take care of his own drugs.

My sessions with Dr. Forrest always get me going, which I suppose is the point. That new pregnant inmate Priscilla gets me going, too. I was trying to think today if there was a moment when things could of went either way.

When I noticed my son wasn't like other children, I thought he was just taking a little more time. My brother was slow like that. Jimmy wanted me to do homeschooling from the start, and he sent away to Bob Jones University where you can get all kinds of textbooks and videos for free. I got cheap kids' books and blocks and puzzles at the Goodwill, and sometimes I wondered if the kids they belonged to were dead—Dr. Forrest would say I have dead kids on the brain.

When we were little, when my real father was gone, but before we moved in with Uncle Dad, my mom used to take us at night to the Goodwill container at the candy factory in East Moriches. She would open the latch and dump my brother and I inside with a flashlight. She figured it was a good way to get things, not just for free, but first look, and it was. It smelled good outside because of the factory, but it was awful inside that container. It smelled like a rotten string mop. It wasn't that easy to get out, either. I did not dump Shane and Kaley into any Goodwill box, just so you know.

Homeschooling was hard. Not knowing Shane had a disability didn't help. One of the signs is the child can't make eye contact with you. I didn't notice at first, and no one else did, either. It wasn't till Kaley was eighteen months old and just before Shane's fourth birthday that the doctor at the VA hospital said maybe we should get him checked out. He had a fit in the doctor's office when he saw a sign of a red Ronald McDonald, which should have been a clue, but it wasn't. We didn't know anything. I'm not saying that as a excuse, just that we were ignorant.

Jimmy prayed all night when the doctor told us, begging the Lord's forgiveness. I was not very religious when I met

Jimmy, but he taught me how to talk to the Lord and, more important, how to listen to the Word. They are very into the Word at the Assembly of God. Jimmy said Shane's sickness was punishment for our past sins. He said it was because we had sexual relations before we were married. At first, I was rebellious in my heart and I thought, Maybe your sins but not mine. And then I remembered about Uncle Dad, and what Ellie had to do for me. Jimmy's and my sins were nothing compared to my own.

Eventually, I gave up trying to teach Shane at home and enrolled him in the local school. I didn't tell them about him cause I wanted them to take him like he was a normal kid. I was hoping they wouldn't figure it out, but of course they did.

I don't know why I can't call her. Not that I'm losing any sleep over it. I like her. She's interesting. And she likes me, which is half the battle. Half the problem.

She was coming through the parking lot tonight just as I was getting into Vinnie Delamar's cousin's car. Vinnie arranged it. Now that everyone knows I'm getting divorced, thanks to Cready, I'm everyone's favorite setup. I had no idea there were so many sisters and cousins, not to mention ex-wives, in the world. I met my wife in college. In those days, guys' sisters were just sisters. You got your own pussy. Anyway, I think she saw me.

I don't know what's the matter with me. It's not like I don't enjoy myself. She's nice to fuck. A little eager, but that can be fixed. It doesn't get really good until the third or fourth time anyway, even with the best. It's not about the fucking anyway. It's more like she makes me nervous. She's not in my league. The idea of me in that fancy apartment makes me laugh. Not that she asked me to move in. And the kid. She's terrified of her kid, which is not a good sign. The other night, she told me she made the boy's father marry her after she got a letter one day from her father, who she hadn't heard from in years. She said she's been trying to make up for it ever since, both to her son's father and to the kid himself, but most of all to the kid. Make up for what? I asked. What? she said, her eyes going a little funny. I could see it was not a conversation she wanted to have—not that I wanted to—and I changed the subject. She sucked my dick instead.

I try to remember Jimmy's face, but I can't always remember what he looks like. I take out his picture, but Shane and Kaley are in the picture, too, so I have to put it back in the box. One thing I can say is I'm happy I never have to have relations again. That part was always hard for me. He had to have intercourse every Sunday. We used to meet after church and do it in his car. I liked it in the beginning, but that's because he did. I didn't feel any personal badness when I had intercourse with him, even if I should of. He thought I was a virgin, and I never told him any different. In some ways I was.

No one knew about us except Uncle Dad. Jimmy didn't have many friends, and I didn't have any friends at all, except for Ellie, and she couldn't stand Jimmy. With Uncle Dad, there was a routine worked out over the years, but with Jimmy things never went so smooth. Once my foot got stuck in Jimmy's steering wheel and I limped around for weeks. Another time, his car rolled backwards down a hill with us inside when he accidentally undid the emergency brake. He couldn't help getting into accidents—it was pretty obvious we'd end up together. With Uncle Dad nothing ever seemed to go wrong, I can say that for him. He was very organized.

I know I mentioned it like it didn't mean anything, but I was pretty upset when my mom told me about Jimmy suing Dr. Kyrgorin. First of all, it was not Dr. Kyrgorin's fault. There is nothing he could of done. No one could of stopped me except the Horsemen themselves. In the beginning, before I understood what they really wanted, the Messengers got me confused. When I tried to hurt myself after Shane was born, it was because I didn't want to do anything bad to my baby. I couldn't hurt my baby. I thought if I did something to myself INSTEAD, he would be spared. The Messengers would be satisfied. But it turned out they didn't want ME. You can't fool the Messengers! The Horsemen are stronger than all of us. Stronger than Jimmy. Stronger than poor Dr. Kyrgorin who got stuck with me when they put me in Marcy the second time. He could hardly speak English. And now Jimmy is suing him cause I did what the voices told me to do. I'd of liked to see him try to disobey Messengers sent by the Lord Himself. My mom says it's all just to get money from the insurance companies and doesn't really matter, but it matters to me. I don't like folks being blamed for something they didn't do.

. . .

was feeling so restless tonight that I walked to the Annex after work. I was hoping I'd run into Bradshaw. I could hear the train to Manhattan rattling through the weeds as it rushed south along the river, and I felt guilty that I wasn't on it, but only for a moment.

The jukebox in the Annex was playing Rod Stewart, which reminded me of boarding school. I ordered a Zin. Two men sitting next to me at the bar were talking about a girl named Nicole. I didn't realize they were discussing Nicole Kidman until quite late in the conversation. One of them, big and very tan, appeared to be hustling a young man in a tracksuit. The young man asked, Why do you think he left her? That's what gets me. And the tanned man said, Who? Tom? Yeah, Tom, said the young man. Didn't she leave him? I thought she left him, said the tanned man. I don't know about adopting kids, said the other man, shaking his head. Could be you're asking for trouble. Not right away, but down the line. I heard she adopted kids because she didn't want to mess up her body, but I don't know. That doesn't seem right, said the tanned gentleman in disgust. No wonder Tom left her.

As I crossed the parking lot, I saw Captain Bradshaw climbing into a Toyota driven by a pretty Hispanic girl. I don't think he saw me. I hope he didn't see me. I hid behind some cars. I felt like I'd been punched in the stomach.

couldn't sleep tonight. The ceremony for making me part of Wanda and Jo's family is tomorrow. Rita offered to do my hair. She's allowed to have a pair of children's scissors with no points for her cosmetology class. Nothing too short or too stud, just a trim. I'll have to watch her cause you know how they do, they take off way too much no matter what you say. They can't help themselves. I asked could I borrow the scissors when she was finished, and she looked at me like I was crazy, but I really only wanted them for my knitting.

I will have four new cousins—Shaynna, Dolores, Blackie (because of his/her teeth), and Linda. It's a little confusing. I don't know yet which cousin is a woman and which is a man, but Wanda says it's not that hard to figure out. Shaynna pulls her T-shirt tight around her waist and ties it in a knot so I know she's a girl cousin, even if she likes girls. I used to feel funny if Shaynna touched me even by accident, like on my hand or my shoulder, but I don't anymore. She is a very nice person.

I received word Saturday morning at home that Priscilla, the pregnant girl in 22, had hemorrhaged to death in the prison clinic. The doctor on call, a locums resident in orthopedic surgery, incorrectly diagnosed a vaginal infection and prescribed Flagyl. She went into labor in the middle of the night. Although the aide tried to reach the doctor, he had turned off his pager. She claims she had no other phone numbers. The baby was stillborn.

I was a little hysterical. Like Dr. de la Vega, I wanted to know why Priscilla didn't call me for help. I tried to find Dr. Henska, who has the Saturday shift, but she didn't answer her phone. I called Captain Bradshaw, but he didn't answer, either. I spent the rest of the weekend on the phone, tracking down the docs. Drinking and crying.

. . .

There's a rumor that that girl Priscilla who was about to have a baby died, and her baby died, too. They say the aide slept through the whole thing. When you are in labor here, they won't give you any medicine except Advil and they chain your ankles to the sides of the bed. This morning, I asked Dr. Forrest if it was true about Priscilla being dead, and she said it was.

I wonder was it a little boy or little girl. They said that girl Melissa, who had her baby in New Jersey during the senior prom, went back inside after giving birth in the parking lot and asked the band to play a Metallica song so she could dance with her boyfriend, but it turned out that was a rumor, at least the part about Metallica. I read in a magazine she's out of jail now.

A lot of the women were crying when they heard about Number 22. She was a young white girl, a orphan from Connecticut Valley Hospital. She was there her whole short life except for a few years before she came here. She got in trouble over some drugs. Later Shaynna said, What do you think they did with the dead baby. She was crying so hard I thought she'd never stop. I wanted to give her a hug, but I couldn't see her from my cell. I could only hear her.

We talked about the dead girl, Priscilla, in group therapy today. The women know what happened. They are convinced that she died while shackled, which is not the case, but they refuse to believe me.

Keesha, grown emaciated with her disease, often sits with one hand thrust down her jeans, as if idly playing with her testicles, but she was so distressed today that she jumped to her feet to march back and forth, grabbing her balls so convincingly that some of the women, myself included, couldn't help but smile. The Korean woman, Kai, said, What the hell's so funny? You think murder is funny? and the women screamed in delight.

Aida told me later that she is filing a suit against the federal government for the shackling of prisoners during childbirth. I began to tell her that I'd help her, but I stopped myself. When I first came to work here, I was alert to anything that might be considered illegal, if not immoral, for the day when I made an anonymous report to Human Rights Watch—anonymous because I would not want to lose my job. After all, I had vowed in girlhood to be useful—useful in a way that would also gratify my small ambition. I once read everything I could find about imprisonment—Jack Henry Abbott, Eugenia Ginzburg, Michel Foucault, Angela Davis. The diaries of political prisoners in Chile. Madame Roland. I listened to the Smithsonian recordings of the work crews at Angola and Parchman. But I don't have time to read now. I don't want to read. And I don't want to listen to chain gangs, either.

I've requested an inquiry into Priscilla's death. It has taken five days for Officer Rossi to find the forms for me to sign, which is an indication of the course any investigation will take. Dr. de la Vega thinks it's a bad idea—not the inquiry itself, but that it comes of my provocation. He says that it's better to originate these things from the inside (an inmate) or the outside (a human rights advocate), but not from the middle—which would be me.

.   .   .

Rehearsals for the Mexican movie start in a month, and I've been preparing. Tequila shooters for starters. Rafael promises he'll help me with my part. You'd think from his name he is Latino, but he really is a Lebanese person from New Jersey. You could've fooled me. He changed his name when he started working in television. The thing about Rafael is he has more interest in things than any man I ever met. I'm not used to it. My brother, and my father, who's dead, never were interested in anything except maybe sports on TV. My dad liked to watch those bull auctions where the guy talks real fast. He got a kick out of that, but that's about it. Sometimes I think I'm going to pass out when Rafael goes on and on about a sword. He collects swords, among other things. He buys a vintage sword or a helmet for a job and then just keeps it when the movie is over. The living room is full of all the things he's collected. He's figured how things work in this town pretty fast, I have to say, considering he only got here a few years ago. When I think where I was a few years ago, I get down on my knees and thank my lucky stars. Even if Rafael drives me crazy sometimes, no one's beating me up, or even making me clean the house. When I think about where I came from, which I don't like to do that much, it's a fucking miracle.

It was quiet in the prison today—Officer Rossi told me that it is very bad luck to say such a thing aloud, and I must never do it.

As I was returning from the file room, I discovered a window shaped like the porthole of a ship. It overlooks the river. The mist clung to the reeds like wisps of silk. I could hear wild geese, but I couldn't see them. There was the smell of the open sea.

I must remind myself, at every turn, that memory is not the truth. My isolation has always led me to imagine things. I have difficulty recognizing false recollections. When I was fourteen years old, my mother and I were sitting at a table on the terrace of Ventana in Big Sur. She was living apart from my father then. I was watching the ocean. She ordered tea and I turned from the water to look at her. Her white skirt was a red flower. My mother hemorrhaged to death before my eyes, and her skirt was the color of a poppy. That is a true memory, I think.

Yesterday Dr. Forrest said something that confused me even more than usual. She said maybe I was Ellie!

I just stared at her. I didn't say a word. I couldn't. I felt sick to my stomach. Sometimes Dr. Forrest talks like SHE is the crazy one. She said, Why don't you tell me more about your friend Ellie. What has become of her? Well, I said, she didn't become a crazy-doctor in a prison, that's for sure. Then she asked if Ellie looked like me. I was so surprised. No, I told her, trying to stay calm, Ellie is a very pretty girl with lovely skin. Not like me at all. Born that way, too. Everything natural. I don't think I ever saw her wear makeup. Which is not to say she is perfect. She bites her nails, but it's from stress—and Dr. Forrest looked at my nails! Ellie can put on weight around the holidays, I said, but she takes it right off again. Some people might say she is a hothead, but only I know how much self-control she has. She can be shy, but then so can I. Shy, but touchy. In the important things, we are like sisters. I don't know what I'd do without her. But I don't LOOK like her. Is that what you wanted to know? Then I burst into tears.

Dr. Forrest just sat there. Her hands were shaking, though.

Officer Cready's Tip for April: Don't wear neckties or scarfs or necklaces. They can be grabbed and pulled and choke you to death. Your pearls, for example.

Last night I couldn't sleep at all, thinking about that joke Shane used to tell—I was just like him, repeating it till I thought I'd explode. He learned a riddle on the school bus one day, and he just couldn't get it out of his head. The teacher even sent a note home with him, and Jimmy said he'd whip him if he didn't shut up. I would never have let him touch him, even if he was driving me crazy, too. It's just one of the things you do when you're autistic. But I was doing it, too, last night, over and over. It's like I was trying to jam my brain with one thought so I wouldn't have any others. I couldn't even remember where I was. I thought I was invisible. Then I thought I was at home. Then I thought maybe I was back in Marcy, but no, I was sitting on the edge of my cot, my ruler in my hand cause I'd just remeasured all my magazines, which took about three hours, repeating in my brain Shane's joke which was, Knock, knock. Who's there? Marmalade. Marmalade who? Marmalade me but who laid you? when Knock, knock, the Helpmates of the Lord arrived.

I hadn't seen the Messengers for a while. About nine months, actually. Since Dr. Forrest came. They used to guide me through the darkness of my days, and I missed them sometimes. Dr. Forrest had me thinking they were gone for good, but there they were as BIG AS LIFE. She even had me wondering if they were real, but when I smelled that terrible smell I knew they were real all right. They slammed through the walls in their flowing black cloaks, their steeds making those horrible snorting sounds, their feet clanging against the walls, striking sparks, and I wondered how could I ever of doubted them. They must of wondered how I could of doubted them, too. One thing I can say is they surely stopped the joke in my head.

I was so surprised to see them I screamed. They themselves are not the silent types, plus everyone in the block was yelling at me to shut up, so it must of been pretty wild. They don't want to hurt you, they don't want to hurt you, I kept screaming. Captain Bradshaw came to the cell and decided to take me right then and there to the clinic. I blacked out in the clinic. The only thing I remember is the aide was wearing a stabproof vest.

Later, on our way back, there was a funny noise in one of the cells, and Captain Bradshaw and me turned and looked at the same time. On a cot was a woman whose face was invisible, but you could see she was naked. There was another naked woman kneeling on the floor in front of her with her head between her legs. The woman on the floor was black. I could tell because the light in the gallery shone off her back in that shiny way that black skin sometimes does. A funny smell came from the cell, not the Horsemen's smell, but another smell, maybe hooch. A pair of legs dangled from the bunk above and whoever was up there had a mirror to watch them cause I saw it flash in the dark.

They were as surprised as we were, a inmate and a officer not usually walking around that time of night. I grabbed Captain Bradshaw's arm. I thought something bad was happening, and I wanted to help them. Stop it, stop it, I said, but Captain Bradshaw was real calm and controlled. He didn't do anything, didn't pull out his flashlight or his cuffs, just undid my hands from his shirt and said in a quiet voice, You-all better get some clothes on, and started walking again, pushing me ahead of him.

I don't know what they gave me in the clinic, but it made me pretty dreamy. I thought about the two inmates I saw. Ellie told me Uncle Dad used to do that to her sometimes. He would take off her underpants but leave on her dress. He'd lift her on top of the kitchen table, sitting her on the edge. He would spread her legs apart so he could kiss her and lick her there. The table felt cold on her bottom. She could see the spot at the back of his head where his hair was going. His hair was a little greasy. He put his glasses next to her on the table and once she softly pushed them off the table with her hand, and he got upset cause he thought she broke them. It was like he knew she did it on purpose. What was awful, Ellie said, is it gave her a tickly feeling inside, not always, but a lot of the time, if he did it right. You see, she learned there was a right way and a wrong way to do it. The right way made her feel like she had to go to the bathroom but was holding it in. Sometimes she couldn't hold it in and once she urinated on his face, and he didn't like it. He was

132

rough with her when he lifted her down from the table and it made her cry. May God's love bathe her in His mercies.

I've had to change the dosage of Helen's medicine. Her hallucinations have returned. This is a setback for her. They are not as severe as in the past (no convulsions), even if she does see men in black hoods on horseback coming through the walls of her cell. She was so agitated by their appearance the other night that she began to scream. Bradshaw took her to the clinic, where the unlicensed aide gave her an injection of one hundred milligrams of Thorazine—far too high a dosage. It will take her days to recover from the medicine alone. These visions always follow her sensation that she herself has disappeared. She doesn't know that she paraphrases William James.

She accepts in sorrow that Ellie was an imagined creature—she appears to accept it—but it is an admission that I have forced upon her. It breaks her heart. Once she turned away from all that she could not understand—now she turns courageously to face all that she still does not understand. Her past is dead to her, her memory too troubled to unravel. It is an unbearable task anyway; perhaps impossible. To explain is always to explain away.

The tension between her conscious self and the self that she has so long kept hidden is so delicate that I am frightened for her. I always knew how dangerous knowledge would be to her, but must I still hold to the belief that her ignorance is equally dangerous? She said this evening as I was leaving, You are helping me know what I know now, not what I knew then, right? What I know now is not a dream, right, Dr. Forrest? And I said, Right.

My mother is coming to see me. It was hard to sleep last night. Dr. Forrest would of said it was because of her coming, but a person on the tier was meowing all night like a cat, and that maybe had more to do with it. I finally got up and stood by the door of the cell. A woman was shouting, Come on you white cunt-licking fat-ass motherfucking honky piece of shit, I'm the queen and we're going to do it my way, and a guard came running. Whatever he did, she settled down.

It's funny, but I never said many swearwords in my life, at least not out loud, and the ones I did say were for Uncle Dad, but since coming here, I really like to hear other people say them.

To tell the truth, when Ransom first came to stay with us in L.A., I thought there'd be a problem. I hadn't figured him into the picture, but we've all adjusted over the last year. When he's here, I have to be more careful, that's all, and the funny thing is it's been good for me. Better food and better habits. We go to bed early and get up early. It makes me a better actor, too, I can tell. Being with such different kinds of people helps me to play different roles in my life for the time when I will have to play them for real.

As a special treat, I let him come in and sit by the tub while I have a bath. We've made it our little secret, and he likes it a lot. I always cover myself with a washcloth just in case, but he's so cute about it he starts asking when I'm going to take a bath the minute he gets up in the morning. I'm good with kids, even if I never want one. They said I was the best salesperson they ever had in the children's stationery department at Neiman Marcus, which is where I used to work, even if I lie and say I was in Furs on Two.

When I first got to L.A., me and my sister Lee found jobs at a day-care center in Studio City, which is where I got giardia. When I went to the doctor, he said, Are you a dog groomer? which freaked me out, as every dog groomer I've ever known was a dyke. No, I said. Do you work in a nursery school? he asked, and because I kind of did, I said yes. It turns out most people who get giardia are around shit all day, animal as well as human, which is why he asked. I was relieved it wasn't because I looked like a dog groomer. My sister and I never went back to the day-care center after that. Lee got a job screening potential embryo rescuers for Nightlight Christian Adoptions, where she works to this day. Her job is to make sure unused embryos don't go to anyone unsuitable like devil worshippers or homosexuals, which I tease her about since she herself has been known to do a little diving. She sometimes fakes the papers just for fun so the embryos end up going to all kinds of weirdos, which I approve of cause it's more like real families.

. . .

When I was being escorted to the Visit Room to see my mom, Shaynna slipped a folded piece of paper in my hand. I never received a kite before—that's what they call letters here—but I knew not to show my surprise, and I hid it in my fist.

I couldn't imagine who would write to me! It's pretty obvious I don't play. When I came here last year, I was shackled to a woman who told me right off she'd been a lesbian for seventy-two months. Now I know what to look for, I can see what she was, but I didn't know anything then. She had short hair and didn't tuck in her shirt. Her collar was turned up in back. She said she was wearing a man's athletic supporter, but she knew they'd take it away from her when they strip-searched us, and they did. She fell asleep, her head on my shoulder, while we were waiting to be fingerprinted. I was so terrified she'd do something to me, I couldn't move.

There was a delay in the Visit Room, and my mother was late. Usually it's the other way around, the inmates keeping the visitors waiting for hours cause they take extra showers and do their hair ten times. It's because we're so excited to have someone visit us. Once I saw a visitor finally have to leave because her inmate didn't get there in time, and her inmate, who was Keesha, had been waiting two months to see her. Today a visitor was thrown out with her newborn baby cause the baby's coat had a little blue hood, and the mother refused to take it off. Hoods are against the rules for visitors. Also anything black in case you look like a inmate.

While I was waiting, I got to read the first part of the letter. It wasn't Shaynna who wrote it, only delivered it. Which was kind of a relief. It was signed Your Honey Bear. I finished reading it when I got back to my cell. Here it is: I would be the smilingest happy face on the Res if I knew you would be my own special friend. You are a part of the chain of my thought. I know you don't have a roommate or anyone you could talk to. There is a rumor they are moving you. Maybe they will put you in my dorm. There's a empty bed here now. I could be the one to open your heart to. Maybe you like it by your lonesome, but if you don't, and if you want me to write, here I am. It's up to you. I don't want to sign this letter till I know how you feel. Your Honey Bear.

When my mom finally passed through inspection, I had just got to the part about her chain of thought. It had made me blush, and my mom looked at me funny and said, What's wrong with you. The reason she was late is she brought me some Oil of Olay soap, which was very thoughtful of her. The soap they give you here has lye in it, and it brings me out in hives, plus I have rashes from my bad diet. She said they had to make sure she hadn't hid anything in the soap like an iron file, which she thought was supposed to be in a cake, but that is her kind of humor, and then they confiscated it anyway. She came all the way on the special prison visitors' bus from Long Island.

The duty officer said, A brief kiss and embrace is permitted at the start and close of this meeting, so I gave her a hug. I told her when I first came here I didn't want to see my stepfather, and she has respected my wishes. When some of the things came out about him, she still wouldn't believe it, even though I had told her over and over again. It was a terrible thing when my mom used to say she didn't want me for her little girl. She told everyone I made up stories. Ellie was so upset she'd get pains in her stomach. We'd have run away, but where could we go? Once we ran out of the house, and Uncle Dad came after us, scream-

137

ing, I am going to get you, I am going to get you! Ellie disappeared for days after that one. They said at the trial he was abused himself when he was a little boy, but the judge ruled it unimportant to my case, and I agreed with him.

The minute she left for work, Uncle Dad would take me to their room and lock the door. He'd press my face into the pillow, and there would be her smell. She had a strong smell. It would still be on me when I went to school, and sometimes even when I went to sleep. It burned me to ashes. Later, I used to have dreams about Uncle Dad doing to my mom what he did to me, and it would wake me up, my nightgown wet where I'd peed on myself. I used to wonder if it hurt her, too, when he stuck it in. In court, I couldn't look at him when my lawyer asked me to say his name. I couldn't say the name either, only point. I knew later from the TV news he was crying like a baby. One thing I wonder is how I let him do it after my kids were born. I lie in the dark and think about that. I went a little crazy, I know. A lot crazy.

It was so loud in the Visit Room I could barely hear my mother. We had to shout across the table. She couldn't stay very long cause we got such a late start. She told me there was a memorial for Shane at his school last month. The principal, Mr. Hernandez, gave a short speech about closure. There were lots of photographers. They are going to do it every year, since so many people from all over the country showed up.

Rafael is the first guy I've been with who isn't into scenes, which threw me at first. I guess you could say I'm just a natural-born performer. He's also the first guy in my life in a

138

creative line of work. At this stage of my career, I feel my life decisions should be based on business, not personal feelings. Rafael makes perfect sense at this point when I'm making that important transition from TV star to artist. I have my standards, unlike my friend Lanny who used to go out with a dermatologist just to get Botox. They'd stop by his office at night after dinner, and she'd give him a blow job, and he'd fill up her face. It was a perfect arrangement until he gave her shots behind her ears for a headache, and she almost died. Plus it made her have a miscarriage. She didn't even know she was pregnant so she wasn't as freaked out as she might have been, but still she cried for days. Unlike me, she wants lots of kids.

I could tell Dr. Forrest wanted me to talk about my mom today. She surely has moms on the brain. She said, Did your mother visit the other day? Even though she knows she did. I said yes and tried to talk about something else, but not the letter from Your Honey Bear, whoever that may be, but Dr. Forrest brought the subject right back to moms.

How did you feel when you saw her? she said. I said, I felt just fine, thanks. My mother has stood by me even though for the longest time she told everyone, the media, and the police themselves, her daughter was incapable of committing a crime. Your mother stood by you? Dr. Forrest said. Yes, I said, I told my mom and anyone else who would listen to me I did it. I never denied it. What would be the point of that. Then Dr. Forrest said, You even said you were going to do it BEFORE you did it, Helen.

I wasn't sure what she meant. If she meant did I think about it day and night, as if demons with knives and burning coals had entered my brain and taken over my thoughts, then she is right. That is why people get confused about whether I knew the difference between right and wrong or not. The prosecution lawyer who was hired to take the children's side in court said I should be put to death not because I was less than human, which I was, but because we should each and every one of us be held accountable, no matter who we are. That was fine with me. She said if you forgot I was a human, then a vote for death was morally WEIGHTLESS, which was when my lawyer jumped up. The other lawyer said I thought my kids were a burden and deserved the ultimate punishment, which wasn't fine.

I always knew what I had to do was wrong in the eyes of the law, but it wasn't wrong in God's eyes. He wanted me to do it. Why else would He have sent the Horsemen to me? I only thank His Merciful Love for giving me the grace to see them and the grace to hear them. I was confused when the jury came back after a record-breaking thirty-five minutes and did not give the prosecutors what they asked for but sentenced me to life imprisonment instead. My lawyer was crying with happiness. I was confused because I thought I wanted to die, and yet for just a second I was happy, too. It's the only time the Horsemen ever let me down.

One day when Rafael was away on location, I left Ransom here alone. I thought it'd be okay. He can always play in the yard or watch TV, so that wasn't a problem. There's a locked redwood fence around the pool, which you have to have by law (not the redwood) in case someone falls in, so I wasn't worried about him drowning. What turns out was a problem is Ransom's a firebug.

I never thought about fire, to tell the truth. Luckily, the Mexican who comes once a week to do what is called yard work (standing around with a blower strapped to his back) was about to leave when he smelled smoke and pulled the burning curtain through the window and stomped on it. He didn't know where to call me, even though Ransom has my cell number and he'd promised to call if there was ever a problem. He said he was afraid he'd get into trouble. Manuel finally just put him in his truck and took him back to Anaheim. I only knew he wasn't at home when Manuel's wife left a message on my machine. I couldn't understand a word of it, but I was at Deidra's house, and I found her massage person and he translated it for me. Manuel brought him back in the morning.

Ransom had a burn on his hand where he tried to put out the flames. Luckily my first part was on that TV series about nurses and doctors in refugee camps, so one thing I know how to do is make a bandage. What was a bigger problem was Rafael. I had to make up something to tell him, or he'd accuse me of neglecting his kid. My story was that PeeWee my parrot got trapped in the curtain and tore it to shreds with his claws and I had to throw it out. Ransom got hurt helping Manuel burn trash, which is against the law in L.A., but Rafael is from the East Coast and doesn't know that. He liked that curtain. Even if it could've been saved, ending up in the pool when Manuel threw it over the fence did not help. It was a shiny material like tinfoil. He took it home from a video shoot he did at a disco.

Ransom said it was so fun being at Manuel's with all the neighborhood kids that he wanted to live in L.A. forever. Which scared me more than the fire. I figured I had to have a serious talk with him, so I took him shopping. We went to Fred Segal where I stole a belt and bought some halter tops. He came into the dressing room with me and gave me advice—he has a really good fashion sense, which he inherited from his dad. We made a pact not to say anything about the curtain until Rafael asked, and I knew he would cause he notices things like that. Ransom promised he would never play with matches or candles or any other kind of fire again, and I promised I wouldn't leave him alone. I made him promise not to tell about that, too. Then we went to the Beverly Center and I bought him his own cell phone so it could never happen again. I told him he could even call his mother on it, though only at night and on weekends. I can write it off on my taxes as a business expense. Ransom Rivera, my new trainer. Ransom's first phone call, since it wasn't late enough to call his mom in New York, was to Manuel the gardener.

As predicted, Rafael noticed the missing curtain. Almost as he came in the door. We nearly didn't see him cause we were blasting Eminem by the pool. I'm not sure he believed it about PeeWee freaking out, but luckily he was distracted by me standing on the diving board where I was giving Ransom a lesson in swan dives, something I learned the month I was in rehab with that Olympic bronze medal guy. At least it got him out to the pool so Ransom could finally show him the backflip he'd been practicing all vacation. I could tell Rafael was tired from work, but still he cheered as if he'd never seen a backflip before. He's a good guy. That he has this fucked-up arrangement isn't his fault. His ex-wife sounds crazy. He once told me she was abused when she was a little girl, which made her paranoid about men. I asked for more details—I'm interested in that sort of thing—but he finally admitted he didn't know anything, it was just a vague feeling he had based on remarks she made about guys. Remarks she made about him is more like it, but I kept my mouth shut. Which made me wonder what ideas he had about me. Not that I was ever abused. Not counting my brother. Just kidding.

My mom wrote to tell me Jimmy is divorcing me. He made a personal appearance to announce it on the Greta Van Susteren show. I should be getting the legal papers any day now. He called my mother to tell her to watch. He said on the show, No matter what problems you have in life, you still don't do anything to hurt your kids. Well, I agree with that.

My mom said she could feel his anger coming right through the screen. She said she doesn't like what Greta has done to her face. She says what you see on TV is what you will always get in real life, and she's worried Greta has ruined her looks. She was more interested in that than in Jimmy and me.

At first, I was really upset, but that's because I was thinking about me. Once I calmed down, I understood of course he'd never want to lay eyes on me again. Why would he. He stood by me as long as he could. Probably even longer than he ever thought possible for a God-fearing man, which he was always telling everyone he was. I don't blame him. It's too much to ask of anybody, God-fearing or not. He never really believed me about the Messengers. It was nice of him to say he did at the trial, but he didn't really. Which is funny, considering he was so into God. I hope he will find happiness. I know I ruined his life. It's not like I'll miss him cause he was never really there, no matter how hard we both tried. I have to at least give him a A for Effort. He did his best. I hate to admit it, but it's kind of a relief it's over.

Ike stopped by for a drink last night. Ransom was visiting his friend on the eighth floor. As I make sure that Ike is gone before Ransom comes home, or awakens in the morning, it means that they have never met. Ike wonders if I have an imaginary child. Those photographs could be of anyone, he said, and I had to agree.

As I rose from bed to dress, he said, You know, corrections guards have an extremely high rate of alcoholism, spousal abuse, and divorce.

Oh, I said, is that a warning?

Then he said, And a lot of infidelity. He lit a cigarette and propped his pillow against the wall. Making himself comfortable. Have you ever had sex with a woman? he asked.

My first thought was that he was hoping for a threesome, and my heart sank—perhaps he wanted to bring a friend the next time. The pretty girl from Marymount. Officer Cready. I sat on the edge of the bed. His question made me feel defiant. I was in love with a woman when I was a girl, I said.

I saw him think about it, and I saw him grow interested, and then a little aroused. He ran his hand across my breast, touching my nipple.

When I was fifteen, I said, brushing his hand aside, and my father had married again, I was sent on a camping trip with four other girls. Our trip leader was Miss Bostwick, the gym teacher at my school. We caught trout and cooked at a campfire. I needed to prove myself, even then. I had to ride the most ornery horse and swim the highest river. I was trying to die, of course, but I didn't have much luck.

Or you didn't try hard enough, he said.

Or I didn't try hard enough.

And? he asked.

And I slept with the gym teacher. In the mountains. It lasted until I went to college.

He was staring at me, but he didn't say anything.

That's all, I said. I jumped up to put on my clothes. There really is something awful in being both naked and embarrassed.

Wanda's real mad at me. She said, I didn't go to all this trouble just so you could get your skinny white ass in trouble. I thought I could count on you.

I got caught passing a kite to Shaynna for my mystery admirer, Your Honey Bear.

There's a right way to do these things, said Wanda, and you did it the all-wrong way. It's my job to tell it like it is, or was, or whatever, and it's your job to do whatever the fuck I tell you. I guess you are just lonelier than I knew. You are such a loser.

Jo had to make a cherry cheesecake just to calm her down.

Later Wanda gave me a demonstration on how to pass a letter, which she says she didn't show me before because she didn't think I was that way. I explained I am NOT, repeat NOT, that way, and never was. It has nothing to do with anything like that. I was just being polite like I was raised to be. She said she's been on the Res a long time and her guts tell her Your Honey Bear isn't the friend for me.

It's not been a good week. Someone even stole my Bible. Which is actually kind of a relief. The minister was coming to see me every week—sometimes twice a week. He must of thought I needed a lot of forgiveness, and he would be right. He's a black man, but that isn't why I didn't care for him. I might have had those kinds of feelings before I came here, but not now. I told him as nice as I could not to come anymore. His feelings were hurt and I was sorry about that, but I don't want to see him again. I don't want his or anyone else's forgiveness. And I don't want Wanda to be mad at me.

In looking through Helen's file today, I found a copy of a letter from a law firm in Beverly Hills threatening a restraining order should Helen persist in harassing their client, a Miss Angelique Grabarsky. Can they have taken in her address?

I'm feeling a little low. I've never told anyone about Miss Bostwick. Other than my shrink, and he doesn't count. It's not easy for me to talk about her. I don't want fantasies about me and Miss Bostwick leaping around in Ike's head, either.

I didn't scream when she woke me, her fingers pushed inside

me, because I didn't want the other girls to know. In the morning, I washed my sleeping bag in the creek before they were awake. The water was so cold my hands were numb. Later, when my stepmother found Miss Bostwick's letters in my bedside table at home, she made my father write to my school. Miss Bostwick was fired, of course. The last I heard, she was working for a white-water river-rafting company in Flagstaff. Seducing young girls on the Colorado.

Cready's Special Easter Tip: If a prisoner wants to kill herself, she will. At a certain point, it's out of your control, so just go with it.

I fainted today when I was taken back to my cell. In our session, Dr. Forrest said Ellie was a form of me I gave birth to, even though I was only a child myself at the time. She said my whole life no one ever told me the truth, and it was hard for me to know what was real and what wasn't. She says I dreamed up Ellie because of what was happening to me! And what was happening to me? I asked. You tell me, she said. And to both our surprise, I said, What was happening to me was Mr. John Scanlon was raping me. There, I said it.

When I fainted—I almost said on the way home instead of on my way back—the nurse said it was due to hunger. She said

147

if I didn't eat they were going to stick a tube down my throat and MAKE me eat. They already talked about it, she said. I promised I would eat in the commissary from now on, but I can just fake it. She said I was anemic, among other things. I wonder what the other things are. When I fell down, the women watching from the gallery cheered.

Dr. Forrest came to see me tonight. She must of been on her way home cause she had her coat on. I guess the nurse told her what happened. She said she wanted to make sure I was okay. She was sweet to me, and I started to cry all over again. She held my hand through the slit in the door until a officer came by and told her she couldn't do that. She said she didn't think my fainting was about food. She squeezed my hand when she left.

I failed with Helen today. She accused me of acting as her mother once did when she refused to believe her. She said that she'd been stupid to trust me. She said that there was terrible pain in remembering, and she didn't understand why I wanted her to suffer. She thought I was her friend. When I said that knowledge would give her freedom, she said, That's a stupid idea in this place. When I told her that she was ill, she asked, Is that why I take the medicine? To keep the Messengers away? It is not about keeping them or anyone else away, I said, because them is you. She asked, her voice rising, I am the voices? Then she demanded to be taken back to her cell. I gave her three milligrams of Klonopin and called the guard.

As she was leaving, she asked, Did I mother my kids? I can't remember. She stopped, and covered her eyes with her hands. What I mean, she said slowly, is did I murder them? The escorting officer took her arm, and she began to cry. A slip of the forked tongue, the officer said.

Rafael says I spoil his kid when he comes to L.A., and I have to try a little harder! That's the thanks I get. He says I buy him too many things.

I never had a thing when I was little, and it's fun to buy things for Ransom. If it hadn't been for TV, I wouldn't even have known you were supposed to want things. No one had anything. Some of the kids I grew up with didn't even have more than one mom or dad, the other being dead or in jail or just gone. What we did have was drugs. I was a bad girl. Once I figured it out, all I did was want things, which didn't make it easy. Still, wanting things is what got me out. If I'd waited, like everyone else was waiting, I'd still be there. My mom waited her whole life, and look what happened to her. She's probably still waiting, for all I know, and she doesn't even know what she's waiting for. She doesn't even know she's waiting. She asked me the day I turned sixteen if I wanted to know who my real mom and dad were, and after I got over my shock I said, Thanks, but no thanks. She said, Well, I never understood why I was supposed to tell you. Besides, I lost the information years ago. You'd have to track them down.

When I was a little girl, I used to daydream I was from a nice family with money and clothes and cars. What's funny is in my daydream we always lived in California, and now here I am, so you see dreams can come true. For all I know, my real mom is a movie star who had to give me away against her wishes. My mom used to say I acted like a princess anyway. As for my dad, she always said he was Ryan O'Neal because of my blue eyes.

I've been feeling a little better. I was sick for a couple of days and just stayed in my cell.

I've really been missing my kids. Even more than usual which is a lot. Maybe because Easter is coming. I always made them really great baskets. I got a lot of my creative materials at Goodwill, sometimes a year in advance because that's when people throw things out—the day after Easter or the day after Christmas. It's really not the kind of stuff you save for a year anyway, unless you're like me. Nice baskets, not too smashed up, and different-colored pipe cleaners, and that funny green grass. I boiled the eggs myself and used those dyes that look like candy pills. I liked the way the eggs fit in the metal holders for dunking. It felt like I was really making something. I always got a little carried away. Jimmy would get mad—he couldn't eat eggs cause of his high cholesterol, and he said I was wasting money. Me and the kids must of eaten a dozen pink and green eggs in a week. They looked rotten, stained all the way through the shell.

Jo got caught stealing last night from the kitchen. She's been doing it pretty regular, but she got a little greedy with

Easter on its way. She has a lot of cooking to do. Her T-shirt was so packed it looked like she had extra breasts. She had a five-pound bag of sugar, three loaves of rye bread, and twenty frozen bagels. It must of been real cold. She was lucky she didn't get sent to ad seg. She has detention instead cause she makes dulce de leche every Friday for the officer who caught her, and he let her off this time.

I have a new patient named Jackie-O, serving a sentence for robbing a McDonald's a few days short of her twenty-first birthday. The McDonald's happened to be on an army base, making her crime a federal offense. She was held in solitary confinement in an army brig for seventy-two hours until she came of age, when she could be charged as an adult. I asked Ike if her detention could be considered legal, and he looked at me and said, You must be kidding.

Jackie-O, who has never heard of Jackie Onassis or, for that matter, John F. Kennedy, suffers from tardive dyskinesia, a side effect of the enormous amounts of antipsychotic medicine she's been given—I've reduced her dosage by half. She is a trouble-maker, rebellious and rude, stirring up the other women, in particular Mary. Mary spends a lot of her day worrying about the various ways she can accommodate her jailers, and to meet a young woman who refuses to accept their terms is very disturbing to her.

Jackie-O, hands shaking uncontrollably, boasted that it was a four-day Jägermeister binge that sent her into McDonald's with a gun (We love our guns, she said) to get four Big Macs for her boyfriend, who is an MP on the base. Was an MP on the base.

I have good news! The warden has agreed to move me to one of the dorm cells. Dr. Forrest says she shouldn't of told me, but she couldn't help it. I hope I won't disappoint her. It would be pretty scary for everyone if the Horsemen suddenly came screaming through the walls in their long black capes. Kind of a funny idea.

I'm pretty excited. Dr. Forrest says I'll be moving sometime next week. I'll be getting a real job assignment. There's a TV. Friday nights they watch WWE *Smack Down!* A lot of the shows are educational, but their favorites are nature programs (I can hear them from my cell, but I can't see them), especially those with animals paired up, like lions against hyenas or lions against antelopes—lions against just about anything, I guess. There is one show called *Eternal Foes* they really like. Wanda said it appeals to her cause there are no limits to her retaliation. The case managers say you don't have to do the anger and life skills classes, but if you don't, they take the TV away. *Raising Emotionally Healthy Kids* is one I probably won't be watching.

One thing I'll get to do when I move is work out in the gym, although I probably won't. Shaynna said they're always threatening to take away the weights cause why should they help inmates get strong. It makes her laugh cause who needs to be real strong when you're real mad. I've been alone for so long this will be nice for me. Dr. Forrest is nervous about it, I can tell.

. . .

A fight erupted in the yard two days ago between the ferocious Darla, who is white, and a black inmate named Ahnjanoo. I was summoned by two delighted officers to try to calm things down—you'd have thought we were attending a new event in the Special Olympics. The yard, a desiccated baseball diamond complete with rusting metal bleachers and a dilapidated wooden scoreboard, is used by the women as a running track.

Darla and Ahnjanoo, previously roommates, had been close friends, and possibly intimate. One of the officers on the night shift, a white man, perhaps offended by their relationship but certainly alert to opportunity, told Darla that Ahnjanoo had been talking trash about her, causing Darla such fury that she attacked Ahnjanoo with a piece of her plastic hand mirror, broken and sharpened for that purpose. Ahnjanoo has been sent to the clinic with a severed finger. A smiling Darla was dragged to ad seg. The finger has unaccountably not been recovered, leading to the rumor that a friend of Darla's is holding it hostage. I've become an admirer of jailhouse humor, although, in this instance, the finger really is missing.

In the group session later that day, Jackie-O was all for resuming the fight, even when the women furiously pointed out that the officer had lied in the hope of starting just such a quarrel. Some of the guards encourage this kind of provocation, goading the inmates to greater and greater violence. Even though the women know this, they fall into the traps set for them. Jackie-O paraded back and forth, despite my requests that she sit down. Kai, one pale arm caressing the other, at last interrupted her to say, Hey, Jackie-O, you stick with your own damn color, no damn problem.

Mary, who was next to me, began to whimper. Jackie-O, her tongue flicking back and forth, lunged across the room at Kai, shrieking, We on *Candid Camera*! We on *Candid Camera*! LizAnn, so distressed as the time for her hearing grows near that she gags at excessive noise, began to vomit.

The funny thing is that we probably were on *Candid Camera*. Bradshaw once asked if altercations ever occurred during sessions. I've been fortunate, but I wondered if one was about to erupt. I rose to my feet, and Mary rose, too, clinging to me tightly. Her support stockings had slipped to her ankles, and I saw that her swollen legs were mottled brown and gray. Her eyes were bloodshot. Her breath was disgusting—it smelled of Pepto-Bismol and garlic. She looked around the room, eyes wild, and, with a convulsive shudder, threw herself to the floor, taking me with her.

I lay there, staring at the dirty ceiling, Mary's hideous legs under me, as I tried to get my breath. I began to giggle. I felt like a young girl. The others began to laugh, too. We were soon screaming with laughter.

Jackie-O helped me to my feet, and we both lifted Mary into a chair. Weak with happiness, I sent them back to their cells. LizAnn later told me that Jackie-O was high on drugs.

I was moved to my new cell on Monday. I'm with Wanda, Larissa, Shirley, a person I don't know named Janice, and Rita, who is another lifer. Rita killed her husband with a crossbow she bought at a garage sale. It didn't help that he'd just come home from Afghanistan. All his relatives were in court wearing American flags. Janice is doing forty days for violating her parole when she went to her ex-boyfriend's house in the Catskills. She has sores all over from shooting liquid dope mixed with meat tenderizer. She thinks she has bugs in her ears, which is a real possibility since there are bugs in ALL OUR EARS and we're not imagining it. The first thing she said to me was, Maybe you can tell me, hon. What does it feel like being straight? I fucking forgot.

I started to tell her, but she walked away.

Shirley, who is a slob, doesn't help the bug problem—the area around her bed is filthy with rotten food and dirty laundry. There are papers and junk everywhere. Stacks of canned food are piled around Wanda's area, too, but that's how she's paid for her services, and at least her cans aren't open. Wanda's going to get Shirley moved. She said in most prisons that kind of behavior wouldn't be tolerated for one second, but the rules are a little different here.

Wanda gets regular supplies of Seroquel from the women who cheek their meds, and the aides sell her pills, too. She buys a pill for fifty cents and then sells it for two dollars. The women like to crush up the pills and snort them. I asked Wanda why they don't just swallow them like you're supposed to, and she said their whole life they've been snorting and that's what they do best. Besides, it's faster. She said, You-all're addicted to drugs, but I'm addicted to cash.

Rafael was in a bad mood when he got home tonight, and I gave him a foot massage out by the pool, which is something he really likes. He has pretty feet, and he takes care of them.

He's superclean, which is more than I can say for a lot of guys I've been with. His feet are long and skinny. I just wish they weren't so brown. It's almost un-American.

He was on an audition today, only he didn't have to read for a part, like I do. He had to sell an idea—which is much worse, he says. He went to one of those bungalows at the Beverly Hills Hotel, which I myself have never been inside, to be interviewed for Lil Stooge's new music video. There were seven or eight big black guys hanging around, and Lil Stooge's mother, who sat all alone at a room service table with a pink tablecloth eating a seven-course meal served by three waiters, two of them white. There was a baby grand piano in the living room with hundreds of pairs of basketball sneakers on top of it, some of them still in the boxes. Lil Stooge was lying on the sofa watching a basketball game on TV, and Rafael was blocking his view. Lil Stooge shouted, Get out of the way, get out of the way! and Rafael moved to the side and stood there for the rest of the quarter while Lil Stooge and his homeys watched the game. They'd taken all the chairs, and there was no place for him to sit down. During the commercials, Lil Stooge would yell at Rafael, You-all want some sneakers? You want some? Take what you want!

It turns out he has a deal with Nike and they'd just sent them over. I was furious with Rafael that he didn't take any, but he said he could buy his own sneakers, thanks very much. The game was finished and Rafael was still just standing there, waiting to get Lil Stooge's attention, when Lil Stooge said to him out of nowhere, I'm not going to remember you, man. The only way I'd remember you is if we all got shot today. And he went into the bedroom and went to sleep. No wonder Rafael needed a massage.

. . .

I've been feeling a little tense lately. I even got in a argument with Rita about making too much noise when she does her exercises. Dr. Forrest said the change from observation to the general population would be hard, and boy, was she right. Still, it's a MILLION TIMES better than before. It's a little like being at home—the only difference is now everyone is moody, not just one or two of your relations.

They wake you at six a.m. Before, if I kept my light out it meant I didn't want breakfast. I could keep my light out all day if I wanted and just stay in bed, but now I get up, shower, brush my teeth, get dressed, and go to the commissary. Lunch is at eleven, but I only pretend to eat. I still have my Sno-Caps, and I sneak a cookie or two in the afternoon if I get hungry. Now that I'm working, I need a little more food to keep me going.

Everyone likes work, not just me. It makes the day go fast. Some of the women are in the machine shop or the laundry, some in the library, some in clerical. The ones with time for good behavior or close to their release date can work outside on the farm. They grow eleven thousand pounds of beans each year, but I wouldn't know about that—they only eat corn and French fries, anyway. Janice, who is a Canadian, used to work for a printer in Toronto, and her job is those green metal signs you see on the highway. I'm working in the bakery. I'm happy about that. I always liked making cupcakes and treats for my kids.

What's new is no privacy. I can see it's hard for the people who are going out together to find a place to be alone. Rita says it's like being a teenager in love except back then at least some-one had a car. Shaynna told me she never had sex in a bed till she got to prison. Sometimes you get under a blanket, and then everyone just looks the other way, or they don't. That is called tenting. It gives me a funny feeling to watch, not that I can see anything. Just the movement and the sounds excite me a little. Everyone else is used to it and they just keep sleeping, or reading their Bible like Shirley pretends to do. I saw Larissa watching the other night, but when she saw me looking at her, she pretended to be disgusted. You have to use the toilet in front of everyone else, too, but that does not turn me on, I can tell you, either doing it or watching someone else go.

Wanda asked if I'd deliver another package to a friend of the family, and I said I'd be happy to. All I had to do, she said, was make sure no one saw me cause it was supposed to be a surprise. I'm good at keeping secrets.

My father, I said to Bradshaw, took me to the Union Club in San Francisco the night before I left for medical school. He told me something that so shocked me, I've dreamed about it ever since. He told me that my mother had been raped as a young woman. Because of this, she had not been able to enjoy the sexual act unless the rape was reenacted. You know, my father said, as much as I loved her, it was absolutely exhausting, having to go through that rape each damn time. In the end, I wasn't the man for her. My heart just wasn't in it.

It was one of the few times that I ever felt sympathy for my father. I thought he was too drunk to remember telling me, and I preferred it that way, but a few years later, just before I met

Rafael, on the anniversary of my mother's death, he sent me an orchid with a note that read, In belated thanks for our talk that night at the Union Club—No Regrets, Daddy.

Ike was staring at me. I know someone who was raped, he said. Actually, I know lots of people who were raped, but this person ended up marrying her rapist.

It was my turn to stare at him. And what happened to them? I asked.

She dropped the charges before the wedding, but the state insisted on prosecuting him. You know how it works. He did his bid, and she waited for him. I think they're still married. They have a couple of kids. It worked out for them.

He made me smile.

You don't believe me? he asked.

I started to answer him—I *did* believe him—but I saw his eyes drift from my face to the doorway behind me. I turned around.

Ransom was standing there, staring at us calmly. Ike, who was naked, leaned forward to pull the sheet across his body. It was he who spoke first. Hello, he said.

I expected you later, I said to Ransom, grabbing a pair of underpants from the back of a chair.

I had a stomachache, he said, his eyes fastened on Ike.

I put on a sweater and took his hand—small, hot—and we went down the hall to his room. My mind was racing. I wondered what he might have seen, wondered what he knew. I realized with a little shock that I was prepared to repudiate Ike, but Ransom didn't give me the chance. He asked no questions. I told him that I would talk to him later, and he nodded and closed his door.

I returned to my room, but Ike was gone. It hadn't seemed long—I've lost my sense of time since working in the prison. He was going to see his daughter, I knew. I sat on the bed to compose myself. I decided I'd talk to Ransom in the morning.

Shirley was lying on the bed with Rita, sucking her thumb like she does, and with her other hand she held a hunk of Rita's hair, poking the tips with her finger over and over again. I started feeling funny. Uncle Dad used to tickle me with the tips of my hair. Sometimes when I woke up my stomach and legs would be dirty. He used to rip my homework when he rolled over on it. He shaved me when I started to grow hair so I would always look like a little girl. That is why I could never undress in front of anyone. My mother used to punish me for locking the bathroom door, but I had to. It's hard to imagine a mother doesn't know what her thirteen-year-old daughter looks like without her clothes, but mine says she didn't, and one reason is I wouldn't let her. The girls at school thought I was a freak cause I wouldn't let anyone see me, even in my underpants. I had to go into a toilet stall to change for gym. Sometimes so it would go faster with Uncle Dad and be over, I would whisper, Fuck me, fuck me. I knew he liked that. Shirley and Rita were rocking on the bed till lights out, and even after that.

· · ·

I invited Ike to go with me and Ransom to Central Park today. I felt I had to do something. I'd not yet spoken to Ransom about finding Ike naked in my bed. I've been cowardly about it.

I haven't wanted to share either of them. I've always found it difficult, if not impossible, to show affection to someone when there is a third person present, even if the third person would be delighted by it. I worry that the witness will love me the less should it be suspected that I have feelings for another. I also tend to like best the person who is next to me, making it somewhat complicated in a group. It is a child's notion of love, I know. The belief that love is a finite essence that will eventually run out holds a certain logic for me even now, even if I am supposed to know better. Despite the duplicitous assurances of their elders, children understand quite early on that love is an expendable resource. Not necessarily renewable, either.

Ike met us downstairs in the lobby. It was cold, the wind blowing from the Hudson. (I think of it as my river now.) We walked across Fifth Avenue and into the park. I was awkward and loud, trying too hard to please. I spoke as if I were conducting an interview. Ransom, sweetheart! Tell Captain Bradshaw about the parrot in California! Ransom's response, sensibly enough, was a grunt.

I suggested that we stop for some cocoa in the café near the lake. We sat at a little table in the window. I was thinking that the day was turning out all right, despite my nerves, when Ransom dropped what looked like a hunk of dried mud into Ike's coffee. I leaned across the table to take a look. Floating in Ike's cup was a horse turd. I could smell it. I thought for a moment that Ike was going to fish it out with his spoon.

To say that I was interested in my son's gesture would be a mild assessment. I even felt a twinge of pride at the audacity of it. Our excursion, meant to diminish the delusional sense of exclusivity I've encouraged my son to feel in regard to his mother, had taken an unexpected turn. When Ike called over the waiter, I asked Ransom to explain himself. I waited for his answer, the model of a progressive adult, but there was none. We'll discuss this later, I whispered.

We trudged home in silence, heads bowed, perhaps against the wind. Needless to say, Ike did not come upstairs. I decided on the way home to give Ransom time to think about his behavior. In truth, I needed time to think about it.

That night, I read a chapter from *D'Aulaires' Book of Greek Myths* to him. When I'd finished, I asked if he had anything he'd like to say about his rudeness to Captain Bradshaw. He yawned and said that he hadn't. He'd been blissfully at peace all afternoon, shaking hands easily with Ike when he said goodbye in the street. Well, I said, I'd like to talk about what happened even if you do not. I said that I was very upset by what he'd done. He nodded as if I'd complimented him, which made me wonder if I had. I asked if he had any feelings about my friendship with Captain Bradshaw. (The pathos of it!) No, he said sleepily. It would be very understandable, I said, if you were confused about things. Especially after what happened the other evening. When you came into my room and Captain Bradshaw was there. You may even be feeling a little angry.

He rolled his eyes and turned on his side. When I heard his breathing change with sleep, I put out the light and crept away, forgetting to lift the drawbridge.

. . .

I t's a shame the yard is so scary cause it's the only place with green grass and fresh air. You can tell who uses the yard and who doesn't. The ones who go outside look much healthier than the ones who don't. The rest of us look like rabbits, all red around the nose and eyes.

Wanda always scares me to death about the yard, even if she herself goes there. She went to a wedding just last week, complete with a white veil for the bride and a marriage license from the printing shop. When I asked Wanda why she could go to the yard but not me, she said I could do whatever I want. It was just friendly advice. What she means, I know, is I might not be too welcome there. There is always a possibility someone might cut me or want to fight. Wanda is the reason no one hurts me, but she can only do so much. Dr. Forrest worries about it, too. It's why the warden didn't want me in a new cell. I understand if the women don't want me hanging around. It's a miracle they talk to me at all.

Shaynna told me Your Honey Bear is a white girl in Building B called Yvonne! She has short blonde hair, natural not bleached. She wears her jeans way down on her hips like a boy. Sounds suspicious, was my first thought. She told Shaynna I was a mermaid, which is funny considering how the mermaid in the cartoon used to talk to me, but then Shaynna said mermaid is street for femme, which was fine with me cause I'd rather be a femme than a stud any day. Shaynna said the reason she told me is cause secrets aren't meant to be kept. That's why they're called secrets. Shaynna pointed her out today in the commissary. She was way across the room, sitting with her friends, all white girls like her. She's pretty. She's not supposed to know I know, so I had to pretend I wasn't looking.

I didn't see it at first, he did it so fast. If I hadn't seen his grubby little hand coming out of his coat pocket, I might've thought it was some fancy thing they put in Central Park cappuccinos, like too much cinnamon. It took me a second to figure out what it was. Shit did not come to mind immediately, I have to admit. When it began to break apart, it began to stink, and then I knew.

I looked at him, half expecting him to look away, but he stared right back at me. She was so nervous she was talking a mile a minute. Which isn't like her. I guess where her kid is concerned all bets are off.

I called the waiter over. There's shit in my coffee, I said. He asked if I wanted him to take it away. No, I said, I think I'll drink it.

I was interested to see what she'd do. Of course, part of me wanted her to twist his arm behind his back and frog-march him across the park, even if I knew she'd never do it. She told him they'd discuss it later. Big surprise. At least she didn't offer to pay the bill. I hope to Christ she's not that way with her patients or she's going to end up dead.

The wind was still blowing when we left, which gave us an excuse not to talk. Not that there was anything to say. I left them in front of their building and dropped in on an old girlfriend who tends bar up in Morningside Heights.

. . .

Wanda gave me her list of rules today.

WANDA'S LAWS AND ORDERS

A. No snitching, that is Number One.

B. Officers on one team, inmates on the other, and never the twain shall meet. It is just a job to them. They lock doors and unlock them. They walk away at the end of their shift.

C. Never get caught with a girl.

D. Never get caught with a guard.

E. No incest.

F. Don't look for trouble but be ready to defend yourself if you have to. If you've been a friend, your friends will be there for you at your back when you need them.

G. Stay out of the yard, unless cleared by me.

H. Do not ask questions esp. about other people's offenses. I don't care what you did so long as you don't do it to me or my homeys.

I. Stay away from anyone who talks to hisself.

J. Watch out for revengeful roommates. They act up right before release.

K. No drug trafficking without permission from Wanda. Use is okay.

I got a week's detention for passing the kite, which means no mail, no telephone, no dayroom, no movie, no gym. Not that I do that anyway. The letter I wrote didn't say a thing, only thanks for writing, but no, I don't think it's going to work out.

I started to explain today to Officer Molina who caught me what was in the letter, and then I remembered Wanda's rule about them being on the other team. Besides a voice inside told me not to say any more.

I haven't spoken to Ike Bradshaw about our terrible day in the park, and he hasn't mentioned it, either. My nerve, as well as my psychiatric training, fails me.

Tonight when I was running the water for my bath, Ransom asked if he could shave my legs. I reminded myself that when he was four, he asked if it hurt very much when they cut off my penis. His interest tonight, however, seemed more avid than practical, more aroused than sympathetic.

There are a million questions I want to ask him, but I restrain myself. It's not discipline that inhibits me, I realize, but fear. I'm afraid of him. I'm afraid of my sadness. Afraid of my fury. I know that he'll tell me too much.

I'm jealous of Rafael's girlfriend. I'm jealous of Rafael. I'm jealous of Ransom. It seems that I like feeling jealous. I'm not jealous of Ike yet, but I can see the possibilities. Ransom leaves for California at the end of the month. I did not let him shave my legs.

. . .

The thing about being in a cell with other women is there is LOTS TO MEASURE. No one has complained yet, which is nice of them. I wanted to measure a really long piece of yarn Larissa was working on, but she got mad and yanked it away from me, which was for the best cause it turns out it went on forever. She is knitting six hundred and sixty-six feet of black wool into a cape because of her interest in witchcraft. It reminded me of the Horsemen. The first two days I measured just about everything I could get my hands on and put the numbers in the new notebook Dr. Forrest gave me. She could get into hot water for giving me things. I wonder sometimes, Does she want to get in trouble? She's in a funny mood these days.

The telephone rang, waking me. At first I could not make out who it was, and then I recognized Rafael's voice. Still, I couldn't understand him. He was screaming, and I thought at first that something had happened to Ransom, until I remembered that he was down the hall, asleep in his fort. Then I thought that Rafael was in some kind of trouble, and I resolved in an instant to do everything I could to help him.

He seemed to say that he was coming to get Ransom. He repeated himself: I am coming to New York in the morning to get my son. He demanded that the perpetrator be denied access to the house. The perpetrator? What are you talking about? I asked. The perpetrator, he said, is your boyfriend.

I still didn't understand. He isn't here, I said. And he's not my boyfriend. I wondered if I was dreaming.

Are you listening? Rafael shouted. This isn't the first time it's happened, Louise. Ransom called us on his cell phone. Your boyfriend chased my son through your apartment with his dick in his hand.

I turned on the light to look at the time. It was two o'clock. Ike had left at midnight. I jumped out of bed and went into the hall, the phone in my hand. I can fix this, I thought, looking around. I can make this all right. My son doesn't have a cell phone, I said.

Just what is it you're not getting? he shouted. Your son has been molested.

It's not true, I said. This is a misunderstanding. It is classic Freud, a primal scene—

He interrupted me. I don't give a fuck about Freud and his primal scene. I never have. Or whatever fucking primal scene's going on at East Seventy-first Street. I'm coming to get him. I'll see you tomorrow. And he hung up the phone.

I ran down the hall to Ransom's room. There was a light in his room. I knocked once and made to go inside, but the door was locked. I called his name, leaning against the door, rattling the knob in my hand, but he wouldn't answer. I thought for an instant of breaking down the door. I returned to the living room to get the fire poker from the fireplace. As I went to the fireplace, I was distracted by lights in one of the apartments across Park Avenue, and the icy glare of a television. I stood in the window for a long time, shivering with cold. Then I picked up the telephone and called Ike.

He was there in half an hour. You got here so fast, I said.

I was still in the city, he said. I stopped by a friend's bar uptown. I saw your number and I thought something happened at the prison.

No, I said. Not the prison. Ransom says you exposed yourself to him.

He looked at me. I saw in an instant that he would not bother to deny it. He looked a little surprised, that's all. He would leave it to me to know the truth. Whatever the fuck that was. I stared at him with something of the fierceness that I longed to find in him, but he had no intention of answering my fury. It made me hate him. I wondered if he was that way with the prisoners—if so, I thought, it may work with them, but it's not going to work with me. Which is when I ran across the room and hit him in the face.

He held me by the hands, if only to spare himself further harm. He once told me that guilty prisoners fall asleep in the holding cell because they have nothing to fear—they know they did it. He let go of my hands to find his handkerchief. I thought the handkerchief was for me, but he held it to the side of his face. Is this what you're like with LizAnn? I heard myself scream.

You don't know anything, he said quietly. When he walked to the front door, I noticed that he was still wearing his coat. I was momentarily comforted by the thought that perhaps I had lost my mind.

I brought Dr. Forrest some cookies I'd stolen from the prison bakery, but she said she didn't want them. She wasn't very nice about it. She told me not to do it again. I KNOW you're not allowed to give a staff member anything of value, but I wouldn't of thought a cookie was what you'd call valuable. They aren't even made with vanilla extra in case we drink it.

I used to make cookies for Shane and Kaley. Their favorite was peanut butter. We made cookies together one of their last days on earth. I was always thinking up ways to keep Shane busy, which got harder and harder as he got older. I taught him how to fake a conversation by asking a lot of questions, which is a trick I myself like to use on social occasions. I tried to teach him not to stand TOO CLOSE to people, but that was another story. He would not do well here, I can tell you. The other kids used to tell him to walk into traffic, or stop up the toilet, or light the flag with matches, and he'd do it. I'm a little like that, too. I did everything the Horsemen told me. Not to mention you know who.

I'd gone to bed around ten as I had a rehearsal early the next morning, and I was a little groggy cause I'd just taken a pill. I thought at first it was Deidra calling, and I wasn't going to answer, but then I saw Ransom's number.

I could hardly hear him. He was whispering, and I had to shout, What? What? which brought Rafael from the other room where he was sketching. He wanted me to give him the phone, but Ransom kept saying on the other end he only wanted to talk to me—it sounded like he had his hand over the receiver—but then Rafael turned on the light and grabbed the phone. I think if Rafael had just let it alone, it might've turned out different, but once he was involved, it got out of control real fast.

We were up the rest of the night. Ransom told his father that a man in his mom's apartment had come after him with a hard-on. Rafael asked if it happened any other time, and Ransom said,

Yes, lots of times. Rafael kept asking him the same questions over and over again until I finally said, He told you that already, and Rafael yelled at me to keep the fuck out of it. It was the first time he ever swore at me.

He told Ransom to stay in his room and lock the door and not let anyone in, even his mother, and he'd be in New York the next day to get him. Then he called his ex-wife and screamed at her and said he was on his way to pick up his kid. Then he paced for the next three hours, talking the whole time and crying. I could hardly understand him at first. It seemed completely real and completely fake at the same time. It *was* real, but still. It was like he was in improv class, and not doing too good. It was all out of proportion. Maybe he couldn't tell the difference anymore. It was like he was losing control all at once to make up for all the years he hadn't.

He said that when he was sixteen years old, his mother found out his father had a whole other family. When his dad said he was on a business trip, he was really with his other wife and their kids. Rafael took a camel's-hair coat and a pair of brown-and-white shoes from his dad's closet and cut the rest of his father's clothes to shreds. Then he took a taxi to his dad's other family in East Orange, New Jersey. His plan was to beat up his father, but the door was opened by a five-year-old boy and two twin girls. One of the little girls had a bad cold, he said, and her nose was running. Everything just fell apart right there. Once he saw the kids, he couldn't even go into the house. He turned around and went straight to Manhattan. That's when he changed his name. He never saw his father again. His mother died a few years ago. He's only been in New Jersey twice since then, and both times it was for work. He doesn't even know if his dad's still alive. Sometimes kids show up on auditions, and he thinks, Is that my sister? Is that my little brother?

All this between sobs, and belts of tequila, and hugs and more sobs. I told him not to jump to any conclusions about his kid, and he said there weren't too many to jump to. His being so upset made me able to be calm. It always works that way—it's just who gets to which mood first. When I said that maybe the kid made a mistake, he yelled that I didn't know anything about it. That's just the point, I said, we don't know anything about it, which is when he ran into the other room and slammed the door.

I went out by the pool and lit a joint. I have to say for all the fucked-up things that happened when I was a kid, no one ever came at me with his cock in his hand—at least not one I didn't want. I'd never seen Rafael so emotional. I usually don't let anybody talk to me that way, not these days at least, not even Deidra, but he was in pain. From what I knew about his ex-wife, which wasn't much, the whole thing seemed a little hard to believe, but you never know. I went back inside and got him to open the door. I didn't say anything except I was there for him and I would do anything I could to help. I think he appreciated it. He knows how I feel about Ransom. I'd never let anything happen to that kid. I can't imagine his mother'd let anything happen to him, either, but as I said, you never know. I gave him a Dalmane, and he fell asleep with his head in my lap.

I got another letter from Your Honey Bear. Here it is: Hon, I never see you in the yard or even at the commissary, don't you walk or eat? The air is nice but I can't say the same for the food.

You should have a little faith in me. I know we never have spoke, but I won't bite. I was lonely all my life but never like in this place. Sometimes I think I'll die of it. It doesn't only have to be about sex for me. Friendship would be enough, so don't get me wrong. I don't fit in with a lot of the people here. At least I finished high school, which I can't say for the others. The majority never had no structure in their life. They were in the street their whole life. I can tell you have not been in the street. The street would eat you alive, little miss! Its lights out now so I'll close for now—my room mates like to snooze. If you ever get moved over here, you better know how to sleep. Your Honey Bear.

I've been thinking about her letter a lot. I don't think it's a good idea to write back. I don't even keep my lawyer's letters— she sends me all kinds of requests, and she's not even a lesbian as far as I know. I still get letters from people outside prison. I used to get thousands, but there's not so much interest in me now. I get proposals of marriage, too, from both men and women, even if I'm already married. I don't answer any of the letters, even the ones with money and photographs of their kids. I do keep the money and pictures, though. I have hundreds of pictures of other people's kids.

In case you were wondering, a dollar bill—all bills, I guess, but I get mostly dollars—measures two and one-half inches by six inches.

Dr. Forrest had some yellow flowers called daffodils on her desk today, maybe to show how spring has finally arrived. She said people think daffodils don't have a smell, but she thinks they do. When I was leaving her office she gave me two, so I guess she's not still mad about the cookies.

·   ·   ·

There's not much that can surprise me, but this did. The little fucker. I wish I'd been flapping my dick at him every chance I got. If ever there was an advertisement for having more than one kid, those two are it. I used to think my mother was a saint, but now I see she was just smart. What that kid needs is brothers and sisters, not to mention a good kick. Still, he's got balls.

She's not going to do anything about it. I'd put money on it. Too bad I can't make some off Cready, but I don't want his nose in my business any more than it is. Besides, I feel sorry for her. I actually have feelings for her. Who'd have guessed that would happen—Cready would have, that fucker.

I have to say I've been outsmarted lots of times—my about-to-be-ex-wife for openers—but never by an eight-year-old kid. He's good. I was a dumb kid. Covering for my brothers and lying for them. Even taking a beating now and then. My mother used to say, Why do you let them walk all over you? It made her mad, but I never minded.

I never minded anything. It wasn't until I left the police department that things started to fall apart. I spent a year at home before I found the job at Sloatsburg. The kid was in school all day. I thought I'd go crazy. I'd never been alone like that before. I come from a big family. I always did something. My whole life I was doing something.

I know people think I took LizAnn under my wing cause she's like a younger sister—at least the ones who don't think I'm fucking her—but the truth is she reminded me of my mother. Right down to the red hair. That same sweetness. The same no sense of humor. My mother would turn over in her grave if she knew what this kid was saying. And then she'd get him.

. . .

Rafael arrived in New York two days ago. I didn't see him, but we spoke once on the phone. He hasn't decided whether he'll bring charges against Ike Bradshaw—that depends on me, it seems. Rafael demands sole custody of our son. It is clearly not in the best interests of the child to remain in my care, especially as my son refuses to speak to me. If I don't comply, Rafael threatens to charge Bradshaw with indecent exposure and the sexual endangerment of a minor.

Although my lawyer advises me that Rafael has no legal right to take Ransom, I've let Rafael take my son to California. They left yesterday.

Janice said she had a real shock to her system when she realized she hadn't been beat in a whole month. She's looking much better, which isn't hard considering what she looked like when they brought her in. She was one big running sore. She said she woke up this morning and said to herself, Hey, no bruises, no cuts, no black eyes. No busted teeth. No one hit me for a whole month! Of course, she said to me, he wouldn't of had to hit me if I'd just let him kill me like I was supposed to. I was only trying to get away from him. It was all my fault, she said, and then she started to cry. She was talking about her dad.

It wasn't your fault, I said. I gave her a big hug, but she wouldn't stop crying. It must of got pretty loud cause Rita in the top bunk yelled, WILL YOU SHUT THE FUCK UP, and

Janice yelled back, Don't you understand? I'm crying now because I CAN, you stupid cunt.

When I think about what Janice says, it stirs things up in me, too. The people in my life who hurt me the most are the people who told me they loved me the most. Not that they really did love me the most, they just wanted me to think they did. Dr. Forrest is helping me to understand that. I don't want that confusion to happen with her or anyone else ever again. Not that Dr. Forrest's told me she loves me, but she acts like she cares what happens to me, not in any bad way, but in a nice way, and it makes me feel funny. I want to talk to Ellie about it, but I can't find her. Dr. Forrest keeps telling me I can't lose Ellie because I AM Ellie. If that is true, I don't have to feel bad for what I made Ellie do. No Messengers, no Ellie, soon there will be no me. I really miss her. Sometimes I even miss the Horsemen.

I can't eat or sleep. With each day, Ransom's position will grow more intractable, making it harder and harder for him to make his way to the truth. Harder and harder to make his way home. To my shame, I realize that I allowed my son to go to Los Angeles because I was angry with him. I told my lawyer tonight to do everything necessary to bring Ransom back to New York. My lawyer pointed out that Ransom would have been going to Los Angeles in a few weeks anyway. It's not his going, I said. It's getting him back that worries me.

My feelings are so volatile that it frightens me. I spend all day at the prison—it doesn't matter now what time I go home. It's as if I'm unable to leave each evening, yet each morning I'm filled with such dread that I can hardly bring myself to walk through the gates. I locked my office tonight and went to the round window in the passageway. The grasses of the marsh were violet-colored in the falling light. There is a small island in the stream, dark with pines. As I stood there, I saw one of Fenimore Cooper's Mohicans dart soundlessly between the black trees. When I was a girl, I liked to imagine that I'd been taken in an Indian raid. A prisoner, raised by heathens.

I called Ike tonight to tell him I'd changed my mind. I was not giving Rafael custody of Ransom. I told him he'd have to hire a lawyer. Doesn't it depend on the boy? he asked. What you've made of him? When I didn't answer, he said, You think that's a mistake?

No, I said. Children tell the truth. Children can be led to imagine things. Children tell lies. When he was silent, I said, You think I've spoiled him. He waited for a moment before he answered, gauging my capacity for the truth, and decided to say nothing. I'm sorry I hit you, I said.

Don't worry about it, he said. He asked when he could see me, and I said that I was very busy. Soon.

I go over and over in my mind the nights that Ike came to the apartment, and what we did and said, and what we drank, and where we drank it, and how we made love. We were very careful. It was inhibiting to know that Ransom was down the hall. Ransom told the lawyer that Ike had tried to hurt him before.

I've been calling Los Angeles every day in the hope of speaking to Angie, but she doesn't answer her phone. I've tried to reach Rafael, but I only get his voice mail. I keep thinking of the child Helen—not mistaken, not dishonest, not imagining anything. Telling the truth.

. . .

Rafael got back from New York yesterday with Ransom. He doesn't seem like a kid who's just been molested by his mother's boyfriend, not that I'd know. Even if Deidra says everyone in Hollywood's been molested, they all seem pretty normal to me, considering, so it can't be that easy to tell. He was quieter than usual, that's all. It always takes him a few days to warm up anyway.

He asked if the parrot could sleep in his room. He promised he wouldn't wash it in the pool like I caught him doing last time. Washing the bird is okay. Just not in chlorine. The bird, which my first husband gave me, has been coughing ever since. I'd be real upset if anything happened to PeeWee. I've never had a pet before. When I was a kid, we weren't allowed to have animals. We were moving all the time cause of my dad being in the Marines. Once I had one of those small little turtles they sell in plastic tubs, but my brother swallowed it on a dare. I told Ransom, and it made him cry, which surprised me cause I always thought it was funny.

Rafael had to go right back to San Diego. The movie starts shooting in five weeks, and they're already four days behind. To cheer Ransom up, I promised to take him to Kmart with Deidra. She has a deal as their spokesperson. In her contract she gets to go around once a month with a shopping cart and take whatever she wants. She doesn't pick the big things like I would— bicycles and teepees and ice-cream makers—but little things like pot holders and flashlights. Personally, I don't get it. She's going to let Ransom push the cart and choose a couple of things for himself. It's nice of her, even if it's not her stuff. We're going to her house for Easter. Each year she hires rabbits for the lawn. They're too hard to catch after the party, so she just pays the security deposit. She says it's her Easter present to the coyotes.

I didn't mention what happened in New York to Ransom, and he didn't mention it, either.

D r. de la Vega once explained to me that there is a phenomenon in this business, as he calls it, known as force drift. It occurs when an interrogator, encountering just the right amount of resistance from his prisoner, loses the ability to restrain himself. Dr. de la Vega is in no danger of suffering force drift, I know, no matter what the pressure, but he is an unusual man. I appear to be suffering the opposite phenomenon. I experience no resistance at all, and I cannot restrain myself.

I saw Helen this afternoon. As I dragged a chair across the cement floor of my office, I heard myself say, I have a little boy named Ransom.

Yes, she said quietly, I thought so. I had a feeling you did.

She said she'd been thinking a lot about kids lately. I tell them stories when I can't sleep, she said. A story about how stupid girls can be, like taking a bite from the witch's apple, or getting into bed with the wolf, even if he looks like your grandmother. But in the end the girl turns out not to be stupid at all. She saves her grandmother! That's the kind of person I'd like to be, she said.

As I listened to her, my eyes filled with tears. She saw that I was crying, and she stopped talking. She doesn't want me to be unhappy, even for an instant. What does your son look like? she asked. I told her. She nodded as if she already knew. She asked me to draw his hand on a page of her measurement book, and I did. To my surprise, I couldn't get it right. I had to draw it twice. It looked much too big to be a child's hand. You'd think I could draw my son's hand, I said. Don't worry, she said, it's not that easy. It's bigger than you think.

I see Angie is supposed to start her new film any day. There's a story in *Prison Days* about Mexican jails, which makes life here look like a luxury hotel, and I'd like to send it to her. She's on Rollerblades with some unidentified little boy at Venice Beach in one magazine and coming out of a store on world-famous Rodeo Drive in another. She looks happy in the pictures, always with a large Starbucks in her hand and wearing sunglasses. Her nails look nice. She's lovely even in those caught-off-guard moments, which they say is the sign of a real star. The little boy reminds me of Shane.

I was on my way to Building A today when the duty officer told me that the captain needed to see me right away. Which captain would that be? I asked, but I knew who it was. He was waiting for me outside the Visit Room. Good afternoon, Captain

Bradshaw, I said. The officer unlocked the west port for us, but Bradshaw had other plans. He took me by the elbow, somewhat firmly, I thought, and turned me in the direction of the elevator. We were going to the second floor. We were going to my office.

I'm expected in the clinic, I said.

This won't take long, he said.

I unlocked the door to my office, and we went inside. I locked the door and turned on the light.

He turned off the light. Why don't you answer my calls? he asked.

I couldn't see his face. The orange light from the passage shone through the pane in the door and made a patch on the cement floor—it looked like a little fire. I went to my desk. He was right behind me. He put his hands around my waist. I've done bad things, he whispered in my ear. He lifted me onto the desk, pushing me onto my back, one hand at my throat. But not this time, he said.

My heels were on the edge of the desk. He pushed my knees apart and pulled down my panty hose. He stood over me, touching me front and back, pushing his fingers deep inside. I was so wet that it made noise. I opened my legs wider. He bent down and put his mouth to me, and I pressed my vagina against him, wrapping my legs around him.

Suddenly, someone shouted my name. There was another shout, and a rattling of the doorknob. I pushed Ike from me and slid from the desk, pulling down my skirt. One of my shoes had fallen under the desk.

What do you want? he said. Just tell me.

I want you, I said as I bent to find my shoe, but I don't think he heard.

I crossed the room to turn on the light. Dr. Fischl's head was framed in the glass. I opened the door. He blushed when he saw Bradshaw. I thought you were being attacked, he said with an embarrassed laugh. Everything okay?

Couldn't be better, I said as Bradshaw brushed past us.

We are always starting from scratch.

B efore my father died in a car crash and I had to leave college and join the police academy, I took a course taught by a French priest who was in the States on a teaching sabbatical. It wasn't a course required for my major, which—it's almost sad to admit it now—was criminal justice. And while it wasn't a requirement, the class seemed to me to be about something that might come in handy someday, considering the line of work I hoped to take up, which was, in those days, the law. Besides, the subject interested me. The name of the class was Beauty and Mortal Sin. How could you not be interested?

There are two things I remember from the course. I remember them because I remember them all the time. Like my first homicide when I was a young undercover. They're always in my mind.

The first thing is that in order to love you have to be able—more than able, you have to be willing—to lose what you love. And you have to be able to live with that. It's what makes love exciting, and it's what makes it worthwhile. The second thing is that you need more than ugliness for sin. It's beauty that makes sin work. And the more beautiful something is, the more satisfying the sin. I didn't really understand it at first. I was eighteen years old, and a little defensive. I was argumentative in class. Father Paul used to look at me and say, The whole point, Mr. Bradshaw, is to strike to your innermost soul—is that what is happening now? Is your heart standing still?

I walked out of class a couple of times, he made me so mad. But I had both those feelings last night. My heart stood still all right. The funny thing is if that busybody Fischl hadn't showed up, she and I would've ended up okay. She liked it, I know. It excited her. And because she's not too experienced in these things, she thought I liked it, too.

I know what she's trying to do. I do it myself. The women, her work, sex, even the kid—she's doing everything she can not to be afraid. She only has the boy, and she's made him her whole life. Or at least she thinks she has. He hasn't made her his whole life. Lucky for him.

When I came to work this morning, there was a note on my desk from Ike. Helen had been injured in an attack by another inmate. She was in protective custody. I ran to find her, doors slamming behind me, breaking the rules that separate those in the know from the assholes, but I didn't care. I never wanted to be on the team. I just wanted to neutralize them in case I needed something someday. As if that were even possible. They hate me as much as I hate them.

She was strapped to a cot in one of the cells used for solitary confinement. Her head was wrapped in bandages, with holes cut for the eyes and nostrils and mouth. Her eyes were closed. A line of stitches ran across her upper lip like a train of ants. She didn't answer when I said her name. I took her hand where it lay at her side, but she pulled it slowly from my grasp, wetting her lips with her tongue to loosen the dried blood.

There was a towel on the bed rail, and I dipped one end into a paper cup of water and held it to her mouth. She was thirsty and sucked on the towel. I untied the restraining straps and slipped my arm beneath her head to lift her, holding the cup to her mouth so that she could drink, the water seeping into the bandage under her chin. What may I do for you? I asked.

May I? May I? she whispered. I think she tried to smile, but I cannot be sure.

I stood next to her bed for a long time. Someone had written LICK MY TATERED CUNT on the wall. The letters had hardened into a glaze. When at last she was asleep, I tapped softly on the door, and an officer unlocked it and let me out of the cell.

Larissa just stood there, waiting while I put a egg on Shaynna's pillow—they're too breakable to put under the pillow. I was thinking I was really glad I'd decorated enough eggs. I was worried all week about it. I even wrapped one with yarn for Larissa cause I knew how sad she was feeling. The night before, Shaynna told me Easter was the day Larissa's daughter burned to death in a fire. When a child dies it is the worst thing that can happen to anyone. I don't know how you keep on living. Well, the answer is you don't. I know it's bad if your parents die when you're young, but a child is worse. When your mother or father die, you're left alone in the world, but at least it's not always your fault.

The way you love your child is not like anything else. It gives you a stomachache of love. I used to think I felt such sadness because of everything that happened to me, but Dr. Forrest says a mother can feel that way even if she wasn't hurt when she was a little girl. I wonder does she feel that way.

I have to stop now. The pills make me sleepy.

It's a miracle it didn't happen sooner. No one will tell the full story for fear of being a snitch, but Larissa attacked her with a pair of scissors when Helen stayed behind to hide some eggs. I found them—Larissa bent over Helen with the scissors in her hand—when I went to call them a second time for the morning count. She dropped the scissors in my hand without a struggle. Death, she said, was too good for Helen. She was pissed she didn't fight back cause then she'd really have given it to her. She said she was trying to cut her face so the world would always know she was the devil incarnate. There was blood everywhere. When I lifted Helen onto the stretcher, she whispered something to me, but I couldn't hear her.

Larissa was taken to solitary. There's a rumor she's going to be transferred to a prison near the Canadian border. Helen's in solitary, too. Right next to Larissa, in fact.

. . .

Helen has been in the dark and airless room for three days now. I arranged for a portable radio to be given to her, and Ike told me that she listens to it. Soft rock.

I asked the warden if she might be allowed to recover in the clinic, where there is light and a little air, and he looked at me in surprise that I dared make any request on her behalf. He doesn't have to remind me of my part in this. He takes my interest in her as excessive, and it makes him uncomfortable. It's distasteful to him. He said that in future any decisions about Helen will come from his office.

I said that I would give him my guarantee that she'd be safe in the clinic. Guarantees are worthless, he said. You should know that by now. Guarantees don't mean shit, doctor. Especially yours. Well, in that case, I said, what could I say to reassure you? We could have dinner some night and discuss it, he said. Yes, I said, without a moment's pause. The next morning, the order came for her transfer to the clinic. I've made a date with the warden for dinner at the end of the month.

I had a brief conversation with Angie on the phone this evening. Ransom still refuses to speak to me. She says they had a nice Easter, considering. Considering what? I asked, but she said she had to go.

The clinic has ten beds and three big stainless-steel drains in the middle of the floor. They say it used to be the morgue. It's probably true—there are big rubber hoses everywhere.

The medicine Dr. Subramaniya gives me for the pain is pretty strong. I've been dreaming a lot, or maybe that is just being stoned, like Tracy says. Tracy's here cause she got rammed in the head in a fight in the yard and has a concussion. We share my pills—Tracy taught me the first day how to hide them behind my teeth. They don't check you that much here. They think if you got this far you're too sick to make trouble. They don't know Tracy. I didn't know her myself until a week ago. She's a schoolteacher in real life. She's here for forty-eight months for having a baby with a student in her social studies class. He was thirteen at the time. She says they're going to get married when she's released—he'll still be under age, but they're going to run away to Mexico. She calls me her Kitty Cat Friend. I thought it was because I was like a little kitty, but it's because the stitches all over my face look like whiskers. Still, she meant it to be nice. She got me to eat a peanut butter and pancake syrup sandwich yesterday, but then I threw up.

Tracy reminds me of the bad girls in my high school. I always wanted them to like me, but they thought I was the weirdo hiding in the bathroom, which I was. It turns out Tracy is nice—maybe they were, too. They probably were. Tracy might be nice because of the pills, but I don't care. I don't mean the pills make me like her, but she likes the pills. She's swollen from all the drugs she's been taking, which she says is complete hell for her love life, which surprised me. She talks all the time about how in love she is with her baby's father, and I thought that meant she wasn't messing around while she was here.

There's a girl here with a broken arm. Another girl named Ahnjanoo who's been here awhile. Darla cut off her finger, and then it got infected. They found out she had hepatitis C when they did her blood test. They won't treat you for hepatitis C if you will be here less than two years, so Tracy said lucky for Ahnjanoo she is going to be here twenty. This place is still run by the state and not a private health company, which is a good thing. At Kirby last summer a girl went into shock and died. She was coming off heroin and they wouldn't help her. The aides said she just wanted attention. Well, yes, I think she did.

I'm pretty depressed I still haven't heard from Wanda, even if she always said she is not the type to call or write. Tracy heard me ask the aide today if I got any messages or anything, and she said, No one cares about you in prison, hon. Can't you get that through your little head? Forget about it!

Tracy herself refuses to be a part of any family here. She says the husbands and wives inside are more fucked-up than the ones outside. Why wouldn't they be, I wanted to know. I didn't say so to Tracy, but I thought Wanda might have made a exception for me, her daughter, even if she always said she was a one-woman show. I can appreciate that, but she meant it in ways I never imagined. Supposedly she is real mad at Larissa for cutting me and swears she'll kill her the first chance she gets, which is why Larissa is being moved to another prison. Still, I'm disappointed not to hear from her.

The tech in the clinic discovered today that the fruit cup on Helen's breakfast tray is stolen each morning to make alcohol. Dr. Subramaniya has begun to feed her intravenously.

I told her it is a miracle she has a tooth left in her head, given her diet, and she smiled and said her father had very good teeth. How do you know? I asked. My mother used to tell me, she said proudly. I never met him, you know. I mean I must have met him once, she said, but I don't remember it. I was just a baby. For whom were you named? I asked. Do you know the story of Helen of Troy? I was named for my grandmother, she said. She had a heart attack during my trial.

I still haven't spoken to Ransom. My lawyer says that he is making progress. These things take time, he said. What things? I asked. Getting a child on an airplane can't be that hard. He said that one reason my son's return is delayed is that he wants to stay in Los Angeles. I am thinking of going to Los Angeles to get him myself.

I didn't write back to Hollywood yet. I wonder what she would think about my accident, not that I would tell her. I really don't care for her to know. I don't want anyone feeling sorry for me, especially her. I definitely don't want my mom seeing me in this condition, so it's a good thing she's moving. I got a letter from her saying she signed a contract to write a book about me. She's using some of the money to move everybody to Tallahassee, Florida, now that my brother's getting out of the service. She must of got a lot. Kelly's wife Sheree and their four kids are already there. She's going to save the rest of the money for the kids' college education. It made me feel a little left out. Dr. Forrest said it is perfectly understandable to feel that way, but she says that about EVERYTHING. My mom's not taking Uncle Dad with her to Florida. She said I would always be in her thoughts and prayers. I would guess I would be in her thoughts if she is writing my life story. I wonder will she put in the part about Uncle Dad having filthy sex with her only daughter while she was snoring in the next room. I wonder will she put it in about the baths.

I haven't told her about Angie.

I've been stopping by the clinic to see Helen. It's also a way to see Forrest. She still won't return my calls. If she's acting this way because she feels guilty about her kid, that's one thing. If she's acting like this because she believes him, then that's a whole other story. Then she's just crazy. The funny thing is I don't have much experience with crazy people, even working in this place. You'd think I would, but I don't. Junkies, yes. Hustlers. Murderers. And my wife, of course. The night she shot me, I actually stood there and watched her do it. I was a rookie. I used to keep my gun in her purse when we went out. I hadn't got used to the way it felt in a holster, but I wanted to have it near me, even if I was off duty. Especially if I was off duty. I hadn't figured how to carry it yet, and she kept it for me with her lipstick and her wallet.

She was eight months pregnant. Her big stomach made the service revolver look small. I was coming in the front door from parking the car. For a split second, I actually thought about taking her down. She claimed—she always claimed—she thought I was an intruder. As Forrest would say—as Forrest *has* said—maybe I was.

. . .

190

Yesterday when Dr. Forrest was here, Captain Bradshaw came by for a visit, which he's been doing lately. Shaynna was here, too, but only for a minute cause she was on her work detail. Captain Bradshaw made me laugh despite my stitches. I noticed Dr. Forrest wouldn't look at him.

I would say I am a changed person in many ways since the day I arrived in this place, but the person who is really changed is Dr. Forrest. She even looks different. I thought maybe she was wearing makeup today, but when I saw her up close I realized she is just different. She gave me a new Bible, and he teased her that she got religion. Maybe I have, she said. I hope not, I said to myself. She seemed relieved when he left.

I haven't finished the mittens I'm knitting for her boy. Maybe she wouldn't even want them—remember how she was about the cookies. I finished the sweater for Angie in shades of blue, and a lovely color called Tender Pink. It is the colors I always imagined a California sky would be. It made me think about sunsets. I wasted a lot of them. I started to wonder what Ellie thought about sunsets, but I stopped myself. I get confused, maybe cause I've been messing with my pills. I'm all mixed up. I keep wondering where am I, but I can't figure out where there is to be. Where am I trying to get to? I think all the time about getting it right. I just don't know what IT is.

When I was doing my fellowship at Bellevue, I had a patient, an obese woman, twenty-eight years old, who liked to take the head of the teenaged female prostitute decapitated by her

boyfriend from the freezer where it was kept to apply fresh lipstick to the lips and arrange the frozen hair as best she could so
that her boyfriend could then masturbate with it, his fingers
stuffed into the hot-pink dead mouth. She committed suicide
by hoarding her meds over a week's time—Xanax, Sinequan,
Tylenol 4 with codeine, and lorazepam. I was not experienced
enough to notice that she had grown increasingly detached over
the previous seven days. I didn't like her, in part, I understand
now, because she was fat. I still wake up at night at the thought of
her. At the thought that it could happen again. It will happen
again—all of it: the murdered girl, the deadly complicity, the
necrophilia, the annihilation. My negligence. My arrogance. It's
happening right now. It was the fat girl's suicide that brought
me here.

Dr. Forrest gave me a tape measure. It's in a little green leather
case with the letters CF on it. I told her a few days ago
the numbers on my own tape measure were worn out, and
today she just showed up with it. When I asked her about it,
she said it was a good-luck charm she always kept with her.
You can still measure, can't you, she said. I like to see you measuring. It means you're happy. She was kidding me a little,
I think.

I've been pretty worried, it's true. There's not enough time
now for everything I have to do. Having all these tubes in me
doesn't help. Thank goodness I finished Keesha's blanket before I came to the clinic. Keesha is dying now. I worry about her

little boy even if she never saw him once he was born. I know she loved him. Everything she did was for him.

I asked Captain Bradshaw today if he would do me a favor. Dr. Forrest wasn't here yet, so we had some privacy. I don't think I could of asked him if she was here. I've never asked him for anything before, but I'd been thinking about it for a while and I finally got up the nerve to do it. I asked if maybe he could get Yvonne, Your Honey Bear, into the clinic so finally we could meet. I've been going over things in my mind and I want to apologize for turning down her friendship the way I did. I've been feeling pretty bad about it. I was afraid like I've been my whole life. He said he didn't think it would be the impossible dream to get her here.

Janice tried to visit me today, but the aide wouldn't let her in. She had some Sno-Caps for me. I really wish I'd of seen her. She wanted to say goodbye. They're sending her to a halfway house in preparation for her release. I'm real happy for her.

When I first came to work in the prison, I was, I admit, excited by the danger and the strangeness. I was fascinated by those particular idiosyncrasies of culture and race that I understood were accessible to me only through observation and study. It was what I wanted—I'd spent most of my life training for it.

This last year has been difficult. I am worn down. The mysterious—once alluring—now merely confuses me. No matter how much I learn, no matter how instinctively sympathetic I am toward the women, and how deeply I still yearn to understand, I know less and less. I'm gullible. I'm condescending. Impatient. The encouragement of alternatives exhausts me. I've failed with Helen. I've failed with my son.

Well, he did it! Yvonne came yesterday. She's blonde, yes, but Tracy says no way is it natural. She brought some books from the library as a excuse, which was nice because Tracy, who, believe it or not, is still here, is really starting to go crazy now that I don't give her all my pills. The book choices were not the greatest. There was one about a Harriet Tubman and *The Making of "Titanic."* Ahnjanoo grabbed the Titanic book right out of Tracy's hand, and Tracy was furious.

Yvonne said everyone is real sorry for what happened to me. No one really liked Larissa, she said, which I didn't know— some people just grew to pretend to like her. Now I feel sorry for Larissa. Yvonne brought pistachio nuts that someone sent her at Easter. I didn't tell her my mouth is too sore to eat them. I just said I'd save them for later when I got hungry. How did you know I wrote the letters? she asked. I admitted it was Shaynna who told me, and she said, I thought so. Shaynna is such a blab. She agreed Captain Bradshaw is a good guy, plus you don't have to have sexual intercourse with him for payment like some of the others. In a men's prison, if a guard is nice to the inmates, he is an outcast, but it's different here.

I could see her trying not to stare at my face, but she couldn't help it. She didn't stay very long. You might even say she rushed out. The whole time the aide kept saying, Hey, Yvonne, stop bothering my patient, but she wasn't. Being gay or not being gay never came up, and I feel proud about that. I told her I was sorry about turning down her friendship. She said she'd come back when she could. It makes me happy, even if I know she won't.

Dr. Forrest says the attack on me had nothing to do with me and all to do with her, Larissa. She had done it another time three years ago to her roommate at Rikers, and yes, they should of known about it. I told her it wasn't her fault or anyone else's. Sometimes when I think of what Larissa did it makes me upset, but mostly I understand—I surely am all over the place with my emotions.

I really miss Ellie. Dr. Forrest says Ellie will always be with me because she is me. How many times is she going to say it? Does that mean I am my best friend now? I asked. You could put it that way, she said. I didn't say anything, but I did wonder, Would a best friend help you to die, or not. Ellie would. I miss her. I miss my friends. It's funny, but the Horsemen didn't come around much when I was with my friends.

I left Ransom alone at the house today while I went to rehearsal, but I came straight home afterward. I wanted to talk to him. I promised him we'd have a real Texas barbecue by the pool— I lived in El Paso once for eight months—which meant ribs and hot sauce and those tamales I love.

I picked up the food on the way home, and we went out by the pool. I let him fire up the tiki torches even though it was still light and despite the ban on matches. He seemed a little manic, but maybe it was just excitement. My entire family was manic, and I can deal with it. After the thirtieth cannonball, though, I thought about giving him a little slug of Tussionex, but I went inside and took it for him instead. He settled down once we started to eat. Barbecue does that, which was part of my plan. I'd had all day to work it out in my mind. I said, very casual, Hey, it turned out pretty good I got you that cell phone, considering what happened.

He nodded, wiping his hands on the roll of paper towels I'd given him.

Did it ever happen before? I asked, not looking at him on purpose. The thing that happened with the man, I mean.

Yes, he said, licking his fingers. Thirty or forty times.

Really? Wow. But really deadpan, like nothing could shock me, which it pretty much can't, but he didn't know that. That is an awful lot, I said. He exposed his penis to you every day?

Not really, he said.

What's weird is I could feel myself getting upset, but not for Ransom. It was his mom I was identifying with, and the poor guy with the boner. If I felt bad, think how they felt.

Sometimes every day, sometimes not, he said. Sometimes more than once a day.

I felt like one of those detectives on *Crime Scene*. I wished I had a tape recorder. Because I didn't believe him. I could tell he wasn't telling the truth. What was weird is it was like he wanted me to know that. What he wanted, even if he didn't know it yet, was for me to get him out of it. I lit a cigarette and went into the house for a little more cough syrup. When I came back he was on his stomach on a Scooby-Doo float in the middle of the pool. Little grease rings floated around him, and I started to scold him, but then I thought, This kid's got enough to worry about.

You know, I said, when I was a little girl, we had this really cute French poodle, apricot colored, and I loved her more than anything in the world. She slept curled up on my bed at night and followed me to school every day. She waited for me outside until school was over so she could walk me home. Maybe my brother was jealous, I don't know, but he tied an old truck battery he found under the house around her neck and taped her little mouth shut and squeezed her down a drain. Poodles are real good swimmers, but she couldn't get out of that sewer. Then he told my father I did it, and my dad came after me with his belt. I was sobbing and sobbing, but no one believed me, not my mother, not anyone. I have had to live with that my whole life. I never even talked about it till now, but I think it's a story you of all people can relate to. I want you to think about it. If anyone knew me, which they didn't, they'd know it was something I could never do. My brother just couldn't get out of it. Once he told the lie, he didn't know how to fix it. And it completely ruined his life. Not mine, his.

I stopped, realizing I was getting a little carried away, as can happen. What's weird is by the end, like with most things, I'd started to believe it myself. I had tears in my eyes. He lay there, his hands folded under his chin, shivering a little as the sun went down behind the hills. Did you make that up about the man? I asked.

Sort of, he said, and that was that.

. . .

The clinic is unusually quiet. The beds on either side of Helen are empty. Ahnjanoo has been sent back to her cell with nine fingers. The girl with the broken arm has been taken to Bellevue under guard after hitting the aide in the face with her cast.

I sit with Helen, sometimes silent, sometimes following her through the maze of her seemingly aimless thoughts. Anything but aimless thoughts. Her maddening guilelessness makes me a little crazy. Sometimes I want to shake her. Or kiss her. My countertransference is right on schedule. Maybe a little late. I don't have much interest in it. But what next? A plan of escape perhaps. I remember the first time that I saw her. She hadn't bathed in days, and she smelled of urine and menstrual blood.

I was trying to get to the holiness, she said today, and now you say it was inside me all along. Did I say that? I asked. Yes, I think you did, she said. Did you mean it? Yes, I said.

She smiled and shook her head. Now you're the one who doesn't make sense. The Messengers don't exist. They never did.

When I said, You're confused, Helen, they existed in your mind, she turned away from me and refused to speak.

Dr. Forrest says I'll get to go back to Number 46 when my face heals, but I know I won't. It's the first time she's lied to me. At least, I hope it's the first time. Still no word from Wanda, and I never heard from Your Honey Bear again. I knew that would happen. I didn't realize till yesterday how bad I looked. I saw myself in the aide's mirror. No wonder Yvonne's never come back. When I calmed down, I thought about it. If that is the worst it will be, that no one can stand to look at me, I can handle that. I have to. I deserve so much worse.

Tracy's gone back to her cell. She stole four tubes of Preparation H to decorate her walls. Before she left she warned me about hiding the pills. If they find out, she said, they'll shoot you full of Prolixin and turn you into a zombie overnight—which some people like, by the way.

I know about that, I said. They used to do that to me in Marcy. I don't like it.

The papers came for me to sign for Jimmy's divorce. I asked if I could see him once before we did this, but I got word back he doesn't want to ever see me again. I don't blame him, but it would of been nice to say goodbye. My mom says he's become a big shot in that group for kids. Thinking about him made me look in my Bible. *For the Lord has called you like a wife forsaken and grieved in spirit, like a wife of youth when she is cast off, says your God. For a brief moment I forsook you, but with great compassion I will gather you. In overflowing wrath for a moment I hid my face from you, but with everlasting love I will have compassion on you.*

What's important to keep in mind, Dr. Forrest says, is that, like other things, like sadness or anger, hopelessness can be very tiring.

Rafael was more of a problem than Ransom, considering I had to break the news that his kid had lied big time. I like the kid, but no way is he living with us. I had to get him out of here and on a plane back to New York, but I had to do it so he wouldn't get into trouble, and so I wouldn't, either. And I couldn't use the poodle story with Rafael. It also meant he'd have to apologize to his ex-wife for getting all crazy and thinking the worst before he had all the facts. I was grateful in the end, though, for everything that happened cause otherwise I'd never have known about Rafael's mom and dad and how deep his feelings really are, and it's helped me to love him even more. He's a very complicated person, it turns out.

I know by now what makes Rafael hot, but I spent the rest of the day figuring the best approach. A lot of people's future was hanging on it. That night when he got home, I locked Ransom's door and put on the peach silk chiffon panties Rafael bought me and the vintage high heels with the round toes, and walked back and forth across the bedroom till I had his attention, which took, I'm sorry to say, about five minutes, but he was depressed. When he finally looked up, he said, Let me see your breasts, which was more scientific than sexy. He talked me into having my implants out six months ago, and he likes looking at the scars. I lifted my arms. He ran his skinny fingers under my tits, and I could see it got to him. There's something I have to tell you, I said quickly. Do you want to smoke a joint? He said sure and got up and began to roll one, making sure our door was closed. Now that we have a voyeur in the family, he said.

That's just what I want to talk to you about, I said. I think you have to call the doctor. The doctor? he asked. Your wife, I said. You have to call her and talk about what happened with Ransom. There's been a mistake. Oh yes? he said slowly, not flaring up or acting like no matter what I said he'd argue about it. Rafael's not like that. I'm used to people fighting, but Rafael is calm, even if he's Lebanese, so I wasn't all that surprised when he just gave a little sigh and sat back in his chair, the unlit joint in his hand. I sat on his lap and told him that Ransom had pretty much made up everything. He saw the man, I said, that part is true, but the man was with his mom, and he was not coming after anyone except the doctor. He didn't even see Ransom. Ransom got scared and he called us and it got out of hand real fast.

I waited a second, stroking myself, so he could take it in. In my acting class, Mrs. Scott talks about having to take responsibility before you can become an artist, but it could apply to almost anyone. All your choices, she says, are meaningful only if you are responsible. And if you are who you really are, then you can't escape responsibility. You don't even want to anymore. I've learned a lot from her. And I know Rafael enough by now to know he's almost there, too. From what he told me the other night about his father, I knew he could pass this test if he wanted. So I had faith in him.

He sat there, tapping one of my nipples with his finger in his absentminded way, and then he said, real quiet, I better call her. I'm not sure it's so good for him here, I said as he got up. Really? he said, looking surprised, and even a little hurt. No, I said, I don't think this is the place for him. Maybe when he's older, but not now. We can't really take care of him.

He was standing naked in the doorway, the phone in his hand, not saying anything. You're not mad at him, right? I asked. No, he said. He went into the other room and called his ex-wife. They talked for a few minutes, and then he came back and gave me the best fuck he ever gave me. Ransom goes home to his mother next week. I told Rafael I'd go along and make sure he got there. Rafael's late with the sets and can't go himself. I also think he isn't that crazy about seeing his ex.

I told Ransom I'd buy him a parrot.

D r. Forrest mailed the letter for me today. I asked Angie to forgive me for everything. She didn't really get what I was trying to say before—I could tell from the things she wrote back—so this time I just came right out and said it: You are my sister. The only reason I myself know is I figured it out from the magazines. My mom denies it. I also figured out it was Uncle Dad who broke my front tooth, not my brother.

It's not Angie's fault she didn't understand, but mine for not being clear, which has always been a problem for me. It's always been hard for me to say what I want. Not because I don't know, but because I do know. I know how bad I am. I always knew I didn't deserve anything. Dr. Forrest would say that is what happens when a child goes through what I did. So maybe underneath I am not so bad. I don't know. Anyway it's too late, whatever I am.

I told Angie everything I know, which isn't much. Our mom put her up for adoption when our father ran off the second time. My brother Kelly and me were already too much for her to handle without another kid to take care of. I was four and Kelly was just two. My mom said she knew she'd go crazy for sure with another baby, and maybe she was right. Later when I started to feel a little funny over my own babies, I asked her about that, but she denied she ever said it. She said she never said a thing about going crazy. It's a shame cause it would have been a help to me if she could've remembered. She said she didn't regret giving up the baby for one minute because she couldn't love a child she didn't really know, even if she'd carried it around for nine long months. I didn't tell Angie that. I could never feel that way about a baby inside of me, even if I didn't get to know it, but who is to judge, certainly not me. If I ever wondered did she do the right thing, just look at Angie's life now and look at mine, and you will have to admit she did. Surely her life turned out a heck of a lot better than mine. I didn't think about it too much before coming here, but I'm not sure my mom felt about me the way I feel about my own kids, and I guess you could say that's a good thing cause here I am, alive.

From what I can tell from the stories in the magazines, and the parts she plays in movies, my sister is pretty strong and can deal with all this. I never would of wrote to her in the first place if I didn't think she could handle it. I gave her our mom's address and telephone number in Florida and now it is up to them. I wrote to our mother and told her what I did, so there wouldn't be any surprises. She doesn't like surprises. It takes her a while to get used to things, as I have learned. My regret is we'll never all be together. I sent Angie some more pictures of my kids. After all, she is the aunt. I hope she won't be too ashamed of us.

I used to think I would die of pain and love before I could ever do what the Messengers told me to do. It is possible to die of love, I know that now. I used to stand at the end of Kaley's crib when I put her down for a nap that really hot summer when I had them in the wading pool all day long, and I'd think, If I just reach out this hand, if I wrap this hand around that little head, I could hold her down. She would not even fight me. Shane was hyper, but I knew in my heart if I did what the Lord was asking me to do, he would not fight me, either. I could hold them both down.

I feel like I've been waiting for something my whole life. The only difference is now I know it will never come. What is surprising is how long it took to figure it out. Look what I have done. The Messengers were in my imagination. How do you explain that. This time, though, I know what I must do. Pray God gives me the strength. *The Lord called me from the womb, from the body of my mother he named my name. He made my mouth like a sharp sword, in the shadow of his hand he hid me; he made me a polished arrow, in his quiver he hid me away. And he said to me, "You are my servant."*

I did what He wanted the last time, and here I am.

I know that it's the fashion now to credit evil as a force in the world, more a political than philosophical fad, abetted by the conservative Christian movement. While I don't hold to this reactionary belief, it would be disingenuous not to admit that I am afraid sometimes. Satan does not roam happily along Park Avenue in a form that is physically threatening, or even visible, but since coming to this place, I have seen evil. I don't think that it is a force in the world that is arbitrary and random, or that it is subjective or specific, or the consequence of sin, but it's here all the same.

Tonight when I left the clinic, the passage was full of a

ghostly light. Beads of condensation, like blisters, covered the walls. I felt as if I were underwater. It was difficult to breathe. Something was going to happen that I could never imagine.

Ransom comes home on Saturday.

The Messengers are always so clear about what they want! No ifs, ands, or buts for the Horsemen. That's how I always wished I could be instead of the confusion my life has been. Dr. Forrest has told me, over and over, that the Messengers are only in my mind. Only! What the Messengers want this time is for me to save Dr. Forrest. I thought maybe they'd forget once they gave me my instructions, but I should of known better. You can't beat the Messengers for knowing what you have to do. They've been screaming and stomping around for days. They want me to kill Dr. Forrest. I know how to do that. *Purge me with hyssop, and I shall be clean; wash me, and I shall be whiter than snow. Fill me with joy and gladness; let the bones which thou hast broken rejoice. Hide thy face from my sins, and blot out all my iniquities.*

I can hear the aide coming now. She doesn't like to stay up, so she leaves my pills on my table. The hard part has been working it out so I don't get too crazy—I've been taking just enough so the craziness won't show. I keep the pills in my sewing bag. Never did I imagine a hobby would come in so handy! My Dr. Forrest pills, the ones for depression and all the other things, plus the pain pills I saved from when Larissa attacked me. I hope there's no mess up this time.

I think about the children so much—the Horsemen have

stirred up a lot of thoughts from that other time. For a long while, I could not remember for the life of me what I did to them. My mind went blank around the time I made the peanut butter cookies my lawyer talked about so much in the trial, saying I would not have made homemade cookies for my kids if I knew what I was going to do six hours later. I don't know. I still can't remember it too good. I know the Horsemen were everywhere that day, wheeling and screaming and pawing the air. The air stank with their hellish smell. They were in the kitchen, knocking everything from the shelves, and they were in the bedroom when I put Shane and Kaley down for their nap, slamming against the walls and striking sparks with their fiery hooves. I was afraid they'd set the house on fire. Their smell made me sick.

Shaynna told me about a little boy in Michigan whose mother drowned him. He fought so hard he got away for a little bit, but she caught him by the ankle and dragged him back. My little boy wasn't like that. He didn't fight. For once in his life he was good. It was like he knew he had to help me. But it wasn't just about being good. He was quiet because he was scared. He didn't move because he couldn't. We were like each other in more ways than one. Kaley didn't try to get away, either. She was too little, anyway. It's like they both knew all along what I had to do, and they wanted to make it easy for me.

They loved me very much. I was running from one room to the other, screaming my head off and vomiting. Shane just sat on the side of the bed, watching me. I told him to lay down like the good sweet child he is, and he did, and I took the pillow in my hands and pressed it down on his little face, counting to a hundred. The baby I cannot remember, except I had such a feeling of joy that I'd been able to save them both after the months of agony and fear that I fainted, which is how they say they found me. I was screaming so loud the neighbors had finally called the police, although they waited for a bit because they thought it was just another domestic argument. I wonder if they had come sooner, but I wonder about a lot of things.

The aide has turned off the light now and gone back to the little room where she watches TV. The sound of it is peaceful. I like to fall asleep listening to it. Everything is ready. I've counted them so many times in the dark, I know each pill just from the shape and feel of it. They surely are my friends tonight. I wish I could thank Dr. Forrest. I would kiss her hands and tell her how much she has meant to me. After Ellie and my kids, Dr. Forrest has meant more to me than anyone.

I think the baby must of thought I was playing a little game with them, like hide-and-seek or peekaboo. Deep inside, they knew it was for their own good. Deep inside, they knew I wanted to save them from this world of sadness and sin.

I hope I will have my dream tonight. I dream I am tangled in long pieces of cloth, like bandages or a Egyptian mummy or like the baby Jesus wrapped in swaddling clothes away in the manger. The way I stop the dream is I imagine the strips unwinding around me. I stand very still and they just fly off. My arms are long and white with no marks on them at all. They've never been cut in my dreams. My arms are beautiful.

Ike came to my office this morning, coming inside without knocking. His face was pale. He seemed so strained, so altered, that it frightened me. He looked a little crazy. Okay, I said, getting to my feet.

Helen's dead, he said.

We went along the tier to the clinic, the yellow-and-brown air of the prison all around us. I felt like I was floating. For once, there was no sound. The inmates had gone to their morning work details, and the cells were empty. A trusty was sweeping the stairs.

Ike locked the clinic door so that no one else could come inside. We were with her for an hour. I stood next to the bed, holding her hand. In her other hand was my mother's tape measure. As Ike removed the tape from her grasp, the aide leaned around the corner of her room and said, You got to wear gloves to do that, Captain.

A red mitten Helen had been knitting was on the bedside table, and her magazines. She'd written my name on top of an old commissary box. Inside were some letters and her new Bible and the measurement books full of numbers. The entries looked like the reckonings of a mad alchemist. Some of the pages in the Bible were marked, and I looked at them in hope of finding a message. There were some. She is my Messenger.

There was something about her in those last days. She was illuminated. Some care had fallen from her. Her face was girlish, and even pretty, her eyes full of a helpless intelligence. She was no longer waiting. I could see that she was worried about me. More than that, she pitied me. Trust me, she said, more than once.

I've been suspended from my position in the prison. There will be an investigation into Helen's death. The aide has reported that Ike removed evidence from the body. She also said that there was something funny about my relationship with Helen, and she'd thought about reporting it several times. She's been given a reprimand. Ike denies that he took anything from the body. What you get is not what you see—as Mary likes to say.

It won't be easy for me to find another position. It's quite difficult to be fired from a prison. It means that you are too crazy even for them. Perhaps I'll register with Shrinks Only. I'm a bad risk now. Dr. de la Vega has been put in charge in my place. He called to tell me. They are fortunate to have him. He is a very good doctor.

There is more than one shock that comes with Helen's death. Helen believed that Angie Mills was her sister. She had been writing to Angie, but only made their supposed relationship fully clear in a letter she wrote to Angie a few days before her death. That Helen's sister might be Rafael's girlfriend has a grotesque symmetry—I may have to change my mind about coincidence. I don't think it is a deliberate falsehood—Helen was incapable of that—but a mistake. Or another delusion. I read a letter in Helen's file from Angie Mills's lawyer in Los Angeles months ago, but the names are not the same.

There are leaks in the press of Helen's surprising relation to the actress Angie Mills. Despite her initial denial, Helen's mother will appear next month with Ms. Mills on a TV show about women who have one good child and one bad child. Angie will meet her purported birth mother for the first time on the show.

The story of Helen's death has occasioned much speculation as to the collapse of medical standards in state institutions. As this is the sixth prison suicide in New York State this year, the press has seized on it as symptomatic of all that is wrong with public health care. As it was Helen, the murderer of her own children, there is some concern that justice should have been cheated of its due. She was supposed to pay the price, and now she has eluded her punishment. Since she may be the sister of a movie star, there is less outrage, however, than there might have been.

My sister left me the rights to her life story. I'm interested in doing a screenplay, but her husband is asking for a lot of money. They're still married. She never signed the divorce papers. A publisher in New York already asked me to write a book about finding out I'm the sister of a woman who smothers her kids. Rafael says I've only got a few weeks to turn all of this into something big, things happening so fast nowadays, and he's right.

When I told my other mom, who's in a nursing home in Elko, Nevada, she wanted to know if she'd get to be on TV. She always did get right to the point. I told her she'd have to work that out with my new mom. She asked if my real dad was Ryan O'Neal, and I thought for a minute about saying yes, just to make her happy, but she'd tell everyone and it would get in the papers and then I'd have to deny it. Not that that would be a bad thing, but my hands are a little full at the moment. I'm grateful the dad who raised me is dead. I couldn't of dealt with him. He'd have turned it into a three-ring circus and tried to find a way to make money out of it. My sister Lee asked if she could play herself in the movie, and I said, Why not. Deidra wants to direct it.

I'm kind of sorry I never got to meet my sister Helen. From

the pictures Rafael downloaded (there were about a thousand), we don't really look like sisters. Even taking in account I color my hair. Which made me wonder for a minute, Were our dads the same? I talked to Rafael about it and Mrs. Scott and the psychic, and the conclusion pretty much seems to be she really could be my sister, whoever the dad might be. Anyway, it would be easy to find out with those DNA tests they give you now. Something deep inside me, even without the tests, tells me it's true. What's really weird is the little dead girl Kaley looks like I did when I was a baby. Deidra says that happens sometimes. She also says it's a big fucking scam.

In all the excitement, I never really stopped to think about what it means to have a mother I didn't even know I had, not to mention a sister who killed her own kids. It's at moments like this I'm grateful for my craft because in all honesty, and it hurts to admit this, I don't feel very much. I felt bad about that at first, but then Rafael helped me to see it's pretty normal. He was great. He said, How could you feel something about people who were complete strangers to you ten minutes ago? Rafael got everything he could find about Helen from the Internet—it will take months to read it all—and I really got into it. She didn't have a chance. It makes my childhood look like Princess Diana. She sounds like she was crazy for a long time. She had no one to help her. Everyone was giving her pills and shock treatments. Her stepfather should be castrated. And her husband. He got her pregnant when she'd already gone crazy with their first kid. It makes me think I'm right about not wanting kids. As sorry as I feel for her, though, I wouldn't have wanted to get too close. These things rub off on you, and not always in the best way.

She wrote me a letter just before she died. She said the more she knew about herself, the harder it was to go on. What is interesting is she took complete responsibility for herself (my new theme). I wondered when I was reading the letter if maybe the only way she could get away from her stepfather was to get herself locked up for life. Which is a scary thought. All I can say is her suffering is over. At least that's what I'll say at my press conference. Mrs. Scott worked with me on it, and I'm pretty prepared. We both decided tears would be too much.

The really weird thing is Rafael's ex-wife was the psychiatrist. I'd have to change that in the screenplay. It's too weird. I hope she likes this guy she's with. The one chasing Ransom down the hall with the hard-on. Sounds like another screenplay.

I took Deidra's advice and put half an Ambien in Ransom's Coke on the plane, and he slept the whole way, which was pretty impressive considering the fucking parrot was screaming the entire two thousand miles. I would've given the parrot the rest of the pill, but I couldn't get his beak open. The man in the seat behind us was very nice about it—I think he recognized me—and when I explained the parrot belonged to a little boy who'd been abused, he didn't say another word about it.

I'd been drinking martinis. I hadn't changed my nightgown in days, although I hadn't begun to measure the furniture yet—I must remember to buy a tape measure—when Ike Bradshaw appeared. It was the first time I'd seen him since Helen's death.

I told him that Ransom was arriving in the morning from California with Angie Mills. They took baths together, I said.

You need a bath, he said.

I'm glad you're amused, I said.

It's you who are amused, he said.

Only by my jealousy. I'm jealous that they took baths together.

No, you're not, he said. He went into the kitchen to make coffee. There's no food, he said. He offered to go to the market if I cleaned up while he was gone, and I agreed.

When he returned with the groceries, I was standing naked in the middle of the living room. Clean. Shirley's in court today, he said, staring at me. I hate Shirley, I said. I could hear him laughing as he put away the food. Come help me, he called, and I did.

Our lovemaking was tentative and delicate. I cried, which may explain the delicacy. In mental health court, he said as he lay back on the pillow, defendants are not allowed to touch their friends or relatives. Certainly not embrace.

Thanks for making an exception, I said. He started to dress and I began to cry again. I'm sorry about what happened, I said. Sorry for all of it.

Don't get carried away, he said. It always gets you in trouble.

I thought, not for the first time, that he really should have been a priest. Perhaps one of the Franciscan friars in the South Bronx with their rough medieval gowns and rope belts knotted three times for poverty, chastity, and obedience, although his belt would have only one knot in it. To my surprise, given the somewhat wide range of my emotions, I took his hand. They're not sisters, I said. I have the records. He began to speak, but

I stopped him. It will come out eventually, I said. But not yet. Let's try to imagine it.

It's the dead, not the living, who give us the worst time. But she knows that. Helen, at the very least, will give her a run for her money.

It will be different at the prison without her. The women will complain. I can't say the warden will. Cready will be heartbroken. Thinking of that made me smile for the first time today.

Only the mysterious can survive. She knows that, too.

The apartment had never looked so nice, it's true. I'd put lilacs in my mother's blue-and-white Chinese bowls and set them in the open windows so their smell would drift through the rooms. Evelyn was there. I was dressed—simply but not severely—in a black skirt and sweater. And patent-leather high heels.

They arrived after lunch. Ransom carried his new parrot in a cage—I believe that he was happy to see me, but it was hard to know. We hadn't spoken in eighteen days. I had a pain in the center of my chest—where my heart would be, as Helen might say. He gave me a tight little smile. Is that all? I managed to ask. He tried again, and the smile was better the second time. Hi, Mom, he said. I was so relieved that my eyes filled with tears. He took one look at me and ran into the kitchen to see Evelyn.

I asked her to sit down. She looks like her photographs—I've been reading Helen's old movie magazines, in which, to my delight, there are several photographs of Ransom. She is prettier in real life, of course. There is nothing incomplete about her. It was a bit of a shock—I've grown accustomed to incompleteness. Her smile is complicit and full of mockery. Her yellow hair was in a French braid, her shining skin taut across her cheekbones. She was wearing pink sweatpants, a white cashmere sweatshirt with a hood, and white high-heeled chamois boots with turquoise beading. She would not have been allowed anywhere near the Visit Room. Ransom returned from the kitchen with a plate of chicken sandwiches. He sat on the floor with it, staring at her in absentminded admiration. It was a habit with him, I could tell. I didn't blame him. She was wonderful.

I'd thoughtfully made a pitcher of margaritas, and I poured her a drink. I'd already had one. I could feel that she wished to speak to me alone, and I asked Ransom to take the sandwiches into the kitchen. He resisted at first, jumping to his feet to stand between us on the sofa where we sat, pressed against either end, but at last I persuaded him by making him feel guilty about Evelyn. He took the parrot with him, and I was left alone with her.

I'm sorry about the mess, she said. I don't know what came over him.

I felt my face flush. She spoke of Ransom as if he were her child. It's my fault, I said, not his. I understand why he did it. I'm very grateful to you for setting it right. Thank you.

I'm glad someone understands, she said, cause I sure don't. I hope it didn't wreck things with your boyfriend. With her speech impediment, the word wreck sounded like weck. She looked around the room. You and me couldn't be more different, could we? It really does make me wonder.

About Rafael? I asked.

About all of it, she said.

I wouldn't, I said. Wonder about it.

Well, I guess you'd know, she said. You're the expert.

Not really, I said.

I wanted to talk to you about that woman, she said. My sister. Did you know her in prison?

Yes, I said. I felt a moment's disappointment that Helen hadn't told her about me.

She gave me a big smile. You think she's my sister, right?

Yes, I said. Lying.

This lady who's supposed to be my real mom, the mom who gave me away when I was born, says she wants to let bygones be bygones. That sounds like someone who could be my mom. She let out a laugh. My agent says I have to do a book before my new mom gets hers out. I might want to interview you for it. She had a sudden thought. You're not doing one, are you?

No, I said. I was very attached to Helen.

Well, she said, it's taken time for it to settle in. It was a pretty big shock, and everything happening at once. It freaked me out at first. My friend Deidra still thinks it's all just a big hustle.

Your lawyer calls you Grabarsky. I found a letter in Helen's file, but I didn't know that it was you.

I think Angie Mills is a hundred times better, don't you?

Yes, I said. I did think so.

She asked what I was going to do about a job. I said that I was thinking about teaching. Maybe I would do volunteer work. I certainly hoped to have friends again. She said that if I ever wanted to write a screenplay about everything that had happened I was to let her know. I thought she was referring to Helen's story, but she said, I've had a pretty unbelievable life.

Ransom came back with his parrot, looking as if he knew he'd missed something. There was one more thing I wanted to ask her, and I asked him to get her a glass of water from the kitchen. When he disappeared with a groan around the corner, the cage swinging wildly, I said, Did he ever watch you take a bath?

God, no! she said. Where did you get that idea?

Before I could answer, he returned with the glass of water. Thank you for Ransom's bird, I said. I hoped she did not hear the dread in my voice. I already could tell that Ransom would not care whether I liked his bird or not. She gave Ransom a kiss, and then, to my surprise, gave me a kiss, and then went into the kitchen to give an enraptured Evelyn a kiss. I'll see you this summer, she said to Ransom. After camp. He looked at me in alarm, but I was walking her to the door and did not meet his glance. He hadn't been told about camp in Maine yet.

Any tips? she asked at the door. For the press conference.

I told her that she didn't need any help from me or anyone else. Her instincts—brutal, fresh, unencumbered—would always see her through. I left out the brutal and unencumbered part. She offered Evelyn a ride to Midtown in her limo, and Evelyn accepted, even though she lives in the Bronx.

After she left, I went to my room and sat on the bed. I felt quite overwhelmed. Some presents Ransom had brought from California were on my desk. They were from Kmart. Things for the bath. A loofah on a long wooden handle, some liquid soap, and a scented candle. I called him from his room.

His door is to be left open as part of our new arrangement. He's not allowed to lock the door, and he cannot enter my room without knocking, although I hadn't had a chance to tell him yet. He stood in the doorway and looked at me, wary of reproach. Wary of everything. Do I still get a story at night? he asked. Of course, I said. He came to me and I took him on my lap. I told him how much I'd missed him. The tension in his body eased a little. I told him that I was sorry there had been an untruth about Ike. A lie about Ike. I did not call it a misunderstanding, as I once did. He was silent, perhaps expecting more, and I had a sudden panic that he was refusing to speak again. I'm glad that you were able to tell the truth, I said. You must be happy about that. He wiggled out of my arms with a little smile. Comme ci, comme ça, he said, and skipped off to his room.

I sat there for a long time. Once I thought I heard Ike's voice, but it was my imagination. I thought about Rafael's feet—slender, long, intensely clean. The feet of Masaccio's dead Christ. He could not stay in bed if his feet were hot. Perhaps those brown-and-white shoes stolen from his father were temperature controlled. Kept his feet cool. He looked after his feet very well. I once caught him oiling them. I miss Rafael's feet, not his cock.

At some point, I telephoned him. I was prepared to leave a message, but he answered the phone. Caller ID, he said. It occurred to me that he might have thought it was Ransom who was calling. He is a good father, even if he, too, has two families. It's not his fault that he fills me with fury. I'd been thinking for some time that I wanted to apologize to him, but the minute I heard his voice I changed my mind. I managed to tell him that I liked his girlfriend very much.

One step at a time, he said, to my surprise. He wanted to

know if I'd read about the arrest of a man in Iowa for killing and eating his dad. I was able to say that I had, in fact, been following the story with interest as I had quite a bit of time on my hands.

I'm sorry, he said then. About Ransom. Sorry about overreacting.

Is that what you call it? I asked.

He wanted to know what I called it.

If I really thought you cared to know, I said, I'd tell you.

He was silent for a moment, perhaps weighing the value of a quarrel. Did you know about the crazy sister? It's your prison.

My prison. I thought about hanging up on him. I could hear Ransom in his room down the hall, singing softly to the exhausted parrot. He'd named it Hercules. He'd put his action figures inside the cage with it. I glanced at the time. Angie would be on the local news, giving her press conference in the ballroom of the Plaza Hotel. Helen would have been proud of her, making the most of her death. I was just beginning to know her, I said to Rafael. I thought we had more time.

All the time in the world, it must have seemed, he said.

I could hear him smile. I thanked him for sending Ransom home. That's all I really wanted to say. He was frightened, I said.

It was Angie who got him out of it, he said. Thank her.

I did, I said. I thanked her. When he didn't say anything, I wondered if he was rifling through a Web site on cannibalism for a topic of conversation. I have to put him to bed now, I said, lying. I'm taking away his cell phone. Just so you know.

Well, he said, I'm glad everything got straightened out. I don't know what I could have done.

Trusted me, I said.

I thought this was about Ransom, he said.

I really do have to go, I said. Genghis Khan is attacking Hercules.

He laughed. I miss you sometimes, he said. Which is when I quietly put down the telephone.

I was surprised to see Rafael's car in the driveway when I got home from the airport. Luckily, I didn't bring Steve Jaffe, who has a deal at Fox, home with me, which he definitely would have done if I'd let him. He was sitting next to me on the plane from New York. I can see how guys in first class are a good catch (*Us* magazine was paying for my ticket), but they must have changed some of the requirements for flight attendants. The ones in our part of the plane were about a hundred years old, besides two of them were lesbians. When I asked Deidra about it, she said, One word: feminism. Besides, she said, a really good catch has his own plane. Guys in first class aren't the same anymore. Not in business class, either. You don't want to waste your time with those schmucks.

Anyway, I was alone when I arrived, thank God. Rafael, wearing a big Mexican sombrero and not much else, was waiting for me with a pitcher of margaritas by the pool, even though it was one of those overcast California days. The haze won't burn off till August, something which still pisses me off. He'd left the set early just to be there when I got home, which is the first time he's ever done anything like that. I think he was trying to show me how grateful he was for what I did. It's not that he's not nice to me; he is, but he's distracted by all his career stuff. He works really hard. I understand cause I'm like that, too. I've told him before that I'd do anything for that kid, and I meant it. Believe me, a trip back and forth to New York in forty-eight hours is not what my skin needed.

He wanted to hear how it went. How Ransom acted. And, I could tell, he wanted to hear about her. The thing is I really liked her. It's not like I thought I wouldn't—I just wasn't thinking about her that much. Before I left, I asked her if I could ask a personal question, and she laughed and said, You mean this hasn't been personal? and I said, I guess I mean real personal. This was after a few margaritas, so everyone was in a pretty good mood. She was sitting on the sofa. She has good legs, that I can say. She was wearing a tight skirt and high heels so I could tell about the legs. Her hair was in a ponytail. She put on her glasses if she needed to look at something, like the clock. I could see she was responsible because she said twice she didn't want me to be late for my press conference, which I had no intention of being. I just wasn't nervous about it, like she was. She said that because she's a shrink, people think she's staring at them all the time and saying to herself, Serial killer, child molester, kleptomaniac, when a lot of the time she's really just thinking about getting to the dry cleaner's before it closes.

What I'd like to know, I said, if you don't mind talking about it, is why you ever married him. You're so different. She looked at me and I could see her deciding if she was going to answer me. And then she said, I was dying of loneliness. I wanted to have a child. I wanted to be a mother. A girl had died because I wasn't paying attention. I was afraid.

Oh, I said, you were pregnant. I knew it.

No, she said. But I was going to be. I needed him for that.

Yes, I said. You can make Rafael do things.

I know. Be careful about that, she said. She jumped up and went to the window. What's really mysterious, she said, is why he married me.

I didn't think it was the right time to tell her he thought she had money. It's true she doesn't look poor, so I can see how he might've got it wrong. Besides, it's hard to tell in New York who's rich and who isn't. Even the salesgirls look good. I've been married, too, I said, mainly so she wouldn't feel bad about confiding in me. I've never been a mom, though. And then I remembered Ransom and I said, At least not a real mom. Rafael doesn't know I was married, so please don't say anything. I can't believe I told you—I guess that's what happens with shrinks. I wasn't scared like you, I was stupid. My ex is in prison. I'll have to divorce him eventually, but I don't want it to come out just yet. He's a real lowlife even if he did buy me a house after his first big drug deal. That's why this news about my sister really threw me—she said from the very beginning she'd keep it a secret, but then she did what she did, and it wasn't a secret anymore. To tell the truth, I'm not sure I'd have kept it a secret. Then Louise, which is what she told me to call her, said what Helen had done had really thrown her, too. She said Helen had been like a sister to her, which made me feel a little weird.

I had the letters my sister sent from prison, and I read them again on the plane. She was telling me all along who she was, but I just didn't get it. It's a terrible thing to say, but I still might not of got it if she hadn't died. I need to turn this whole thing

222

into something good, or it could mess me up. I got this far and I really can't afford it right now. I've worked hard not to be messed up. When I got home, I asked Rafael if he wanted to read the letters, but he wasn't that interested in them. What he wanted to know, I could tell, without coming right out and asking me, was what his ex-wife said about him. I don't think she ever got over you, I said.

Really? he said, smiling.

How could she, I said, and I did what I do best, even if the horrible Iranians who live next door were sitting up on their deck, watching what pretends to be a sun disappear behind the hills.

I miss the women, and Helen, so much. I wonder what they are doing every minute of the day—Dr. Fischl will be starting his rounds, clicking open and closed his ballpoint pen. Bradshaw, sweet smelling, sighing, tells LizAnn that he'll miss her, and she answers, a bit tartly, that she's not out yet. Officer Rossi glides noisily down the gallery, having destroyed the last of the evidence necessary for an investigation into the death of the pregnant girl. Dr. de la Vega, his black suit shiny with use, is taking a much-needed nap in his car—he'll be at the prison till midnight tonight. Darla, enraged that her new friend, Tracy, did not keep her promise to save her a front-row seat at the Monday-night movie, refuses to leave her cell. Tracy, stoned on the medicine she stole from Helen, missed the movie thanks to important business she had with Wanda.

Kai is on her hands and knees, scrubbing the floor of the chapel, filthy with Kool-Aid powder and other mysterious substances after the movie last night. No one thanks her for her good housekeeping, but then she does not expect or need praise. Besides, she will earn a dollar and fourteen cents today. Later this afternoon, Officer Cready will tiptoe gracefully into the utility closet to keep his weekly appointment with her.

Shirley, her conviction overturned, has gone home. Keesha lies near death in Kirby Hospital. Mary, diagnosed with diabetes, is in the next cell, unaware that Keesha is dying next to her. Jackie-O, intent on stealing Wanda's position as drug queen, sharpens the homemade knife she will use this evening to attack Wanda in the shower. Officer Molina, high on crystal meth, will save Wanda's life tonight, and not for the first time.

Helen's corpse, on its way to Los Angeles now that Angie Mills, in the company of several television crews, has claimed the body, will arrive just in time for the evening news shows. There will be a private funeral for her next month at the Resting Place of the Stars Memorial Park in Burbank.

Here, in this world, Ransom is washing his parrot in the sink. I may, or may not, see Bradshaw this weekend. It depends on whether his wife will let him say goodbye to his little girl.

A NOTE ON THE TYPE

Pierre Simon Fournier *le jeune,* who designed the type used in this book, was both an originator and a collector of types. His types are old style in character and sharply cut. In 1764 and 1766 he published his *Manuel typographique,* a treatise on the history of French types and printing, on typefounding in all its details, and on what many consider his most important contribution to typography—the measurement of type by the point system.

Composed by TexTech,
Brattleboro, Vermont
Designed by Wesley Gott